James Hadley Chase (born René Brabazon Raymond) was born in London in 1906. He worked as a bookseller during which time he was inspired by American crime-writers and went on to write his own thrillers and gangster stories, also set in the United States. He first found success with *No Orchids for Miss Blandish* which was published in 1939 and was one of the most successful books of the thirties, selling several million copies. George Orwell described it as 'a brilliant piece of writing with hardly a wasted word or a jarring note anywhere'. It was subsequently dramatised and performed on London's West End and also made into a film. Chase went on to gain popularity for his numerous other gangster stories, and by the end of the war he was one of Britain's most successful thriller writers. During his career he produced some ninety books, also writing under the names of James L Dochery, Ambrose Grant and Raymond Marshall. He travelled widely, though only visited the USA late in life. He died in 1985 whilst in Switzerland.

BY THE SAME AUTHOR
ALL PUBLISHED BY HOUSE OF STRATUS

An Ace Up My Sleeve
An Ear to the Ground
The Fast Buck
Goldfish Have No Hiding Place
The Guilty are Afraid
Hand Me a Fig-Leaf
Have a Change of Scene
Have This One On Me
Hit and Run
Hit Them Where it Hurts
Just a Matter of Time
Knock, Knock! Who's There?
Like a Hole in the Head
Make the Corpse Walk
More Deadly Than the Male
My Laugh Comes Last
Not My Thing
So What Happens to Me?
Tell it to the Birds
The Whiff of Money
You're Dead Without Money

JAMES HADLEY

CHASE

You Have Yourself a Deal

This edition published in 2000 by The House of Stratus, an imprint of Stratus Books Ltd., 21 Beeching Park, Kelly Bray, Cornwall, PL17 8QS, UK..

www.houseofstratus.com

Typeset, printed and bound by The House of Stratus.

A catalogue record for this book is available from the British Library and the Library of Congress.

ISBN 1-84232-119-6

Cover design: Marc Burville-Riley
Cover image: Photonica

1

Captain O'Halloran parked his Jeep in one of the bays in the courtyard of the United States Embassy, picked up a black leather briefcase on the seat beside him, slid his big frame out of the Jeep and walked briskly up the steps leading into the Embassy. He nodded to the man behind the reception desk, took the elevator to the second floor, walked down a corridor, climbed six stairs to another level as a tall, well-built woman of thirty-five or six came hurrying towards him. She was Marcia Davis, PA to the Head of the Paris Division of the CIA. Her face lit up with a smile as O'Halloran paused. Her grey eyes ran swiftly over him. His red, fleshy face, his shapeless nose, his light blue eyes and hard mouth always gave her a slight sinking feeling. She often speculated what it would be like to be gripped in those thick, muscular arms.

"Hello, Tim," she said. "What are you doing here?"

"The old man in?" O'Halloran asked, also speculating how this attractive red-headed woman would react if he were ever lucky enough to get her into his bed.

"When isn't he?" she returned. "You'll find him ... come the day you don't. Have you had your vacation yet?"

"Vacation? What's that?" O'Halloran asked, grinning. "I'll be lucky if I get Christmas off. How about you?"

"September ... I've booked on a Cruise. See you, Tim," and with a flashing smile, she hurried on.

O'Halloran looked back and watched the challenging swing of her hips, put on, he shrewdly guessed, for his own special benefit. Then jerking his mind back to business, he continued on down the corridor to a door on which was inscribed in gold lettering:

Central Intelligence Agency
Divisional Director John Dorey

The lettering was sparklingly new and O'Halloran grinned, shaking his head in awed admiration. So finally Dorey had made it, he thought. There had been a time, not so very long ago when the Division had been running a sweepstake on Dorey's chances of survival. That was when Washington had sent Thorley Warely over as Head of the Division and Dorey, after thirty-eight years of service at the Embassy, had been relegated to second place. But now Warely was back in Washington and Dorey, although over sixty years of age, had taken on a new lease in life. He was a man O'Halloran admired and liked: a man who took risks, short cuts and had vision.

O'Halloran rapped, opened the door and walked into the comfortable office where Dorey was sitting at a vast desk, reading a file.

Dorey was a small birdlike man, wearing rimless glasses. Always immaculately dressed, he looked like a successful banker rather than the Director of the CIA. He dropped the file on his desk, eased back his executive chair and looked at O'Halloran over the tops of his glasses.

"Hi there, Tim, I haven't seen you in weeks. Something come up?"

O'Halloran kept the door open and jerked his thumb at the gold lettering.

"Congratulations, sir."

Dorey smiled a wintry smile.

"Thank you. Shut the door and sit down." He picked up a gold fountain pen and studied it as he went on, "Everything comes to those who play the right cards at the right time."

"I must remember that, sir." O'Halloran took off his service cap and sat down in one of the big lounging chairs grouped in front of Dorey's desk.

"I was heading for retirement," Dorey went on as if talking to himself, "then Robert Henry Carey* appeared on my landscape and that altered things." He lifted his shoulders. "A stroke of fate. Sometimes we get the right card ... more often not." He laid down the pen and looked directly at O'Halloran. "Well, Tim, what is it?"

"I had a handout from the Sûreté this morning," O'Halloran said, zipping open his briefcase. He took out a file and laid it on his knee. "I thought you should hear about it."

Dorey rested back in his chair. He put the tips of his fingers together and formed his hands into the shape of an arch. This was his favourite listening stance.

"Go ahead."

"Two nights ago, evening of the 4th, a man, parking his car on the Quai de la Tournelle, saw a woman lying in the shadows. He called a gendarme who was passing. The woman was in a coma. An ambulance was called and she was taken to St Lazare hospital. They were full up. The woman was wearing a scarf decorated with the Stars and Stripes and a coat with a Macy label. This was excuse enough for her to be loaded back into the ambulance and taken to the American hospital." O'Halloran paused to consult the file.

* See *This is for Real.*

"So far this doesn't particularly interest me," Dorey said with a note of impatience in his voice.

"The woman was found to be suffering from an overdose of barbiturates," O'Halloran went on in his gravelly cop voice, ignoring Dorey's interruption. "She was treated and put into a ward. She surfaced the following day and was found to be suffering from acute amnesia. She has no idea who she is, where she lives ... a complete memory blank. She speaks fluent English with an American accent and is in a distressed, nervous condition. Hers is not a unique case, of course. Quite a number of people get some form of amnesia. Dr Forrester who is in charge of her ward was anxious to get rid of her. Beds are in demand at the hospital. He gave a description of the woman to the Sûreté who thinking it possible she was either Swedish or Norwegian contacted those embassies without success."

"What made them think she was either Swedish or Norwegian?" Dorey asked.

"Apparently she looks as if she comes from Scandinavia: blonde, tall ... a typical type."

"She had no papers with her?"

"No. She didn't even have a handbag."

Dorey moved impatiently. "Well?"

"I received the usual Sûreté handout about her this morning." O'Halloran looked at the open file on his knee. "Here is her description: blonde, exceptionally good-looking; blue eyes, heavily sun-tanned, height five foot seven, weight 126 lbs." He paused, glanced up at Dorey. "Marks of identification: small mole on her right forearm, and three Chinese symbols tattooed on her left buttock."

Dorey stared at O'Halloran, then picking up his fountain pen, he rubbed the gleaming gold against his thin nose.

"Chinese?"

"That's right. Three Chinese symbols." O'Halloran put the file on the desk. "Well, sir, there is a file somewhere in your Division which came around to me about ten months ago for information. Its subject was Feng Hoh Kung, the top rocket research man in Peking. I remember, amongst a lot of useless information, it was stated that this guy is a little crazy in the head. He likes to put his initials on everything he owns. It is said his initials are on his house, his car, his horse, his dogs, his cooking pots, his clothes, his shoes ... and the women who serve him. I remember too it was said that a year ago he acquired a Swedish mistress. He has three initials. There were three symbols that could be his initials on this woman's bottom. So ..." O'Halloran stretched his massive frame and smiled at Dorey. "I thought you should hear about it."

Dorey sat motionless.

"Who else has this handout?"

"The British Embassy, the Scandinavian Embassies and *France-Matin*."

Dorey winced.

France-Matin was a newspaper he loathed. If there was any hint of trouble, any germ of scandal this paper invariably made capital out of it.

"Did the Sûreté give the handout to the press?"

"I stopped them in time."

"But *France-Matin* has it?"

O'Halloran took a newspaper from his briefcase and handed it across the desk.

"They have it," he said.

On the second page was the headline: *Do You Know This Woman?* Below the caption was a badly reproduced photograph, taken by an uninspired police photographer of a blonde woman who could be any age from twenty to thirty who stared fixedly out of the smudgy newsprint. But in spite of the crudeness of the reproduction, her beauty came through.

Dorey grunted as he read: *Chinese symbols, as yet to be translated, have been found tattooed on the mystery woman's body.*

"How did they get hold of this?" he demanded angrily.

O'Halloran lifted his shoulders.

"How does a vulture find a meal twenty miles away?"

Dorey leaned back in his chair. He thought for a brief moment, then he said slowly, "This could mean nothing I suppose: a lot of women ..." He stopped and shook his head. "Three Chinese symbols! No, this is too much of a coincidence." He sat upright. "Tim, we'll treat this as a top level operation. If we are wrong, we are wrong, but if this woman ..." He drummed on the desk. "What action have you taken so far?"

O'Halloran settled more comfortably in his chair.

"I have taken precautions." He spoke with the confidence of a man who knows his job. "It so happens General Wainright is in the hospital for a check-up so that gave me the excuse to put a guard in the corridor. Wainright and this woman are on the same floor. I have called Dr Forrester and warned him she might be a security risk and no nurse unless known to him should attend to her. The guard has instructions to let only the nurse in the woman's room. I have alerted the reception desk to refuse any visitors calling on her."

Dorey nodded.

"Nice work, Tim. Okay, you can leave this to me. The first move is to find out just what these symbols are on the girl's body. If by some extraordinary bit of luck she is Kung's mistress, she becomes more than a VIP, and we'll be answerable for her. Get out there, Tim. Make sure nothing goes wrong while I get this organised."

O'Halloran got briskly to his feet.

"We could be wasting our time, sir."

"But if we aren't?" Dorey smiled. "I'm lucky to have a man like you working for me. Get moving. I'm starting something this end."

As O'Halloran left the office, Dorey thought for a moment, nodded to himself and reached for the telephone.

In a dingy courtyard off Rue de Rennes, there is a small restaurant called *Le Temple du Ciel*. It is not to be found in any guidebook although it serves the best Chinese food in Paris. Should any tourist discover the restaurant, he would be told with a sorrowful smile that all tables had been reserved. *Le Temple du Ciel* was strictly for the Chinese.

While Dorey was talking to O'Halloran, Chung Wu, the owner of the restaurant was sitting behind the cash desk, supervising his team of waiters as they served lunch to a couple of dozen or so habitués, hidden behind high silk screens that surrounded each table. The clatter of Mah Jongg tiles, the raised voices and the blare of swing music made a deafening noise without which the Chinese feel isolated and unhappy.

The telephone bell shrilled. Chung Wu picked up the receiver, listened, spoke softly in Cantonese dialect, laid down the receiver and walked to a table where Sadu Mitchell was about to begin his lunch.

Sadu's chopsticks were hovering over a dish of King-sized prawns done in a light, golden batter as Chung Wu appeared around the screen. Chung Wu bowed, then turning slightly, he bowed to the Vietnamese girl who sat by Sadu's side.

"Regrets, monsieur ... the telephone ... immediate," Chung Wu said in his atrocious French.

Sadu uttered an obscenity that made his companion giggle. He threw down his chopsticks and waved Chung Wu away.

Sadu Mitchell was tall, slim and thin-faced. His jet black hair was taken straight back, his clothes were immaculate, his almond-shaped eyes were as hard as jet beads. He was the illegitimate son of an American missionary who, thirty years ago, had been a conspicuous failure in Peking. When he finally came to realise that he was making no impression on his so-called flock, he found consolation in whisky and an attractive Chinese girl who considered it her duty to help relieve the stress and strain of his unsuccessful fight to convert the heathen. The result of her administrations was Sadu – half-Chinese, half-American – who resented his illegitimacy so bitterly that he had come to regard the United States of America as his personal enemy.

For the past ten years, Sadu had made a successful living from a small *boutique* which he owned on the Rue de Rivoli where he sold jade and expensive antiques to American tourists. He was a man lost without a woman. During the past year he had found, after several discards, a Vietnamese girl who called herself Pearl Kuo whose beauty completely captivated him as it was meant to captivate him. He discovered her hatred of America made his own bitter dislike a pale and flabby affair. She had lost her family and her home during an American air attack in North Vietnam. She had fled to Hanoi where she had become an agent working for the Chinese. They finally sent her to Paris. Before long she had persuaded Sadu that it was his duty to work also for the Chinese movement. Since he was in constant touch with Americans in his shop, she explained to him, he had the opportunity of picking up scraps of information which he was to pass on to Yet-Sen, an elderly Chinese who worked at the Chinese Embassy. Sadu found this amusing since it gave him the chance to damage American prestige. It was surprising how Americans talked when in a foreign country as if they imagined no one around them could understand English, and sometimes their indiscretions were startling. Sadu's scraps of information helped to feed the Chinese propaganda machine. He felt he was doing something tangible towards levelling the score against his father who had died some ten years ago. What he didn't realise was that he was being carefully groomed for more important and more dangerous work. Pushed gently by Pearl and drawn carefully by Yet-Sen, Sadu was about to reach the point of no return.

This telephone call was to make him into a fully-fledged agent.

Pushing aside the screen, he walked to the telephone and picked up the receiver.

"Yes? Who is it?" he demanded impatiently, thinking of his cooling prawns.

"I am at your shop. Come immediately." He recognised Yet-Sen's guttural voice.

"I can't come now. I ..."

"Immediately," and the line went dead.

Sadu cursed, then returned to his table. Pearl looked inquiringly at him.

"Yet-Sen," Sadu said, his face dark with fury. "He wants to see me at once."

"Then you must go, cheri."

"I'm not his damned servant," Sadu said, hesitating.

"You must go, cheri."

Sadu was now so under her influence that he hesitated no longer.

"Well, wait for me here," he said. "I shouldn't be long," and he left the restaurant.

It took him a little under ten minutes, driving his small red TR4 aggressively through the heavy traffic to reach his shop. As he pulled up, a fat Chinese who had been staring sightlessly at the jade displayed in Sadu's window turned and moved to the car, got in and said quietly, "Go somewhere where we can talk."

Sadu edged the car out into the traffic and drove rapidly down the Rue de Rivoli. He battled his way around the Concorde and started down along the Quai.

Yet-Sen said, "This is an emergency. You have been chosen to handle it. It is a great compliment. Find space to park in the Louvre gardens."

Sadu felt a qualm of uneasiness. He glanced at the fat man, sitting in his thick city suit, his yellow face blank, his small hands, like ivory carvings, folded across his bulging stomach. He drove into the gardens and found parking space, as it was lunch time, in front of the Ministère des Finances and turned off the car engine.

Yet-Sen took a copy of *France-Matin* from his hip pocket and handed it to Sadu. He tapped the badly reproduced photograph of a blonde woman.

"By tomorrow morning this woman must be dead," he said. "We have every confidence in you. You will have all the necessary help, but you must arrange the details. At six o'clock this evening a man will call on you. He is the weapon ... he has no brains. You are to be the brains. Now, please listen carefully ..."

Sadu sat motionless, his thin, long fingers gripping the steering wheel of his car and listened. This became his moment of truth. He suddenly realised that his petty hatred of America, the chip he had carried so long on his shoulder had finally come home to roost. He wasn't certain whether to be pleased or dismayed by this sudden change in his status. But he instinctively knew whatever his reactions, the job would have to be done.

London's Bond Street has a particular fascination for tourists. Even when the shops are closed at the early hour of 5.30, people from all countries of the world will continue to walk down the traffic-congested street and shop-window gaze, admiring old prints, the leather bound books, the linen, the expensive cameras and the de luxe gifts displayed at Asprey's.

Among the stream of people moving down Bond Street at the cocktail hour of 7 p.m. was a giant of a man wearing a shabby, foreign cut suit, scuffed shoes and a Marks & Spencer shirt and tie. This man had silver coloured hair, cut close, a square-shaped face, high cheekbones and flat green eyes. His age might be between thirty and forty, but not more. His muscular body was a shade under six foot five. His sun-tanned face was relaxed and expressionless. He walked easily with the light step of a trained fighter, his big hands thrust into his trousers pockets.

This man whose known name was Malik was Russia's most successful agent. He had been in London now for a week. He had been told to look at the City, get the feel of it and to behave like a tourist. It was possible he might have work to do here.

So Malik was relaxing. He was staying at a small nondescript hotel in Cromwell Road. He was fully aware that MI6 was watching him. He was also aware that his own people had a man following him. All this Malik accepted with indifference. It was part of the game, and he regarded his job as a game, exciting, satisfying and which pandered to his sadistic instincts.

This evening, strolling down Bond Street, he was satisfying his suppressed longing for possessions. Every now and then, he would pause before a shop window and stare with his flat green eyes at the various luxury articles he longed for but knew he could never possess.

There was a portable roulette set that he would have liked to own. In another corner of the window, temptingly displayed, was a leather-embossed blotter complete with a silver and onyx pen set that beckoned to him the way an impossible-to-buy toy beckons to a child. He stood staring through the window of the shop, his face disciplined into a blank mask, his big knuckled fist clenched out of sight in his pockets.

Unwillingly, he moved on, walking slowly, fighting the temptation to stop and look again at things displayed so blatantly in the windows, but now mindful that there was someone following and watching him, ready to make a report, jealous of his reputation, more than willing to ruin him.

The faint sound of a touched motorhorn made him look sharply towards a cruising Jaguar that had slowed to a crawl and was only slightly ahead of him.

A girl was at the wheel: blonde and smiling, not more than twenty-three, a mink stole around her shoulders, her eyes inviting, the lines around her mouth etched deeply in worldly awareness and sin.

Malik looked away. He walked on. He felt the blood move through his body. He had a sudden impulse to go with this whore and show her how a Russian can reduce a woman to a gasping, moaning animal, flattened beneath muscle and sinews. The urgent need to do this brought sweat beads out onto his forehead, but he kept walking, mindful of the unseen watcher, knowing every move he made, good or bad, would be reported, if not tonight, then later.

The Jaguar swung to the kerb as he passed and the girl said softly, "Why be lonely, darling? We could have fun."

Malik kept on. The luxury articles in the shop windows had suddenly lost their fascination. He wanted now only to return to his hotel. Four walls, a curtained window and a locked door offered him the sanctuary he felt in need of, away from watching eyes.

The Jaguar gained speed and passed him. He watched it go with regret. As he reached Piccadilly, the electronic pulser he wore on his wrist, disguised as a watch, began to throb. This was a signal that he was wanted. Immediately he became alert, the fleshy desires, the envy of luxury wiped from his mind. He touched the winder on the pulser to stop the pulse beat, then walked swiftly down Piccadilly to the Berkeley Hotel. Ignoring the stare from the top-hatted doorman, he entered and moved around the groups of chattering people, cocktails in their hands, to him overdressed and stupid looking, to the telephone booths. He gave the attendant a number, again ignoring the man's obvious disapproval of his appearance, then when the man pointed, Malik shut himself in one of the booths. It smelt of some expensive perfume and he thought for a brief moment of the blonde in the Jaguar. His big fists clenched. It would have been good to have shown her how a Russian takes a woman. The telephone bell tinkled and he lifted the receiver.

A man's voice said, "Hello?"

"Four and two and six make twelve," Malik said, using his own special identity code.

"You are to leave immediately for Paris," the man told him in Russian. "You are booked on flight 361, leaving at 20.40 hours. Your things have been packed and are waiting for you at the Air Terminal. S will be at Le Bourget. This is an emergency." The line went dead.

Malik paid for the call and then, leaving the hotel, he picked up a taxi and was driven to the Cromwell Road Air Terminus.

A fat, suety-faced man who was known to Malik as Drina was waiting in the reception lobby. He had with him Malik's shabby suitcase, his ticket and 300 French francs.

"You still have a little time," Drina said. He spoke respectfully. He was a great admirer of Malik, wishing he had the talent and the drive that had established Malik as the top agent. "Is there anything else I can do? I packed your things carefully. Smernoff will meet you at the other end. He would appreciate some duty free cigarettes." The suety face grimaced into a smile. "I thought I could mention it."

Malik hated this fat, dumpy man as he hated anyone connected with failure. He had had dealings with him before and his servile, fawning manner irritated him.

Wordlessly, he took the suitcase, the ticket and the money, then walked away. He knew the watcher was still watching. It wouldn't do even to swear at Drina.

When he arrived at Le Bourget airport, he went through the police control without trouble. His false passport was in order. He was travelling as an American subject on vacation. The police at the airport were used to Americans. They considered that America threw up an odd assortment of breeds. This Slav looking man was just another visitor, welcomed only for his dollars. Malik passed through the barrier and walked out into the big reception hall where Boris Smernoff was waiting. Malik was glad to see him. Smernoff knew his job. He had the reputation of being the most clever and ruthless hunter of men and Malik had often worked with him. He was thickset, dark and heavily built with a bald patch, narrow, cruel eyes and a talent for accepting any difficulty without protesting. His philosophy was: if it is possible, it will be done; if it is impossible, it can be done.

A few minutes before Malik's arrival, there had been a sudden scene of violence. Three young beatniks, dressed in leather jackets with dirty nondescript faces had appeared suddenly and had converged on a man who was sitting inoffensively by the barrier where the passengers from London would arrive. One of them had hit this man over the head with a gutta-percha cosh and then before anyone could act, they had run out, bundled into a shabby Simca and had driven rapidly away into the rain and the darkness.

The assaulted man was one of MI6's Paris agents, alerted by London that Malik was arriving. He had been taken away in an ambulance and Smernoff who had organised the assault was confident that there was no other watcher to see Malik arrive.

As Malik crossed the hall towards Smernoff, Smernoff's thin lips moved into a smile.

"Did you bring me cigarettes?" he asked as the two men shook hands.

"You can poison your own self," Malik said. "Why should I want to hasten your death?"

"You think of no one but yourself," Smernoff said, shrugging. "I have never known you to do anyone a favour."

Malik grunted.

But as they walked out of the airport, he found himself considering this remark. It irritated him to find it was true.

The two men got into a 404 Smernoff had parked in a parking bay. As Smernoff set the car in motion, he said, "This could be a tricky one. A woman has been found suffering from complete loss of memory. She is at the moment in the American Hospital. It is thought she is the mistress of Feng Hoh Kung. We have orders to take her from the hospital to a house already prepared at Malmaison. You have been selected to take care of the operation. American Security know who she is and they have already put a guard on the hospital. It is also possible in a few hours, she will be moved somewhere less accessible."

"They think she has information?" Malik asked.

"They think she might have."

For a few moments Malik sat in silence absorbing this assignment. It appealed to him. He liked action and walking into a hospital which was guarded and taking a woman out, then getting away, was the kind of job he knew he was good at.

"Have you done anything yet or have you waited for me?"

"The matter is urgent," Smernoff said. "I have a man watching the hospital and reporting back every ten minutes. It seems to me the quickest way of getting her is to walk in and take her. We are lucky. An American General, in for a check-up, is on the same floor as she is. I have American Army uniforms, a Jeep and an ambulance at readiness. If you don't like this idea, you will say so. This is your operation: not mine."

Malik glanced at the hard, cruel face of his companion and his eyes glittered. Smernoff was his assistant. He took orders. Malik wondered how much longer that would continue if Smernoff began using his brains so efficiently. He had outlined a plan that Malik would have made. Malik knew this.

"You think like me, Boris. It is a pleasure to work with you. This is a good plan. It should work. I'll see you get the credit."

Smernoff laughed.

"No, you won't," he said, "but if the plan meets with your approval I am glad to pass it on to you. Credit means nothing to me. Why should I care about credit?"

"You are not ambitious, Boris?" Malik asked.

"No ... are you?"

"I wonder sometimes. No ... I suppose I'm not."

Smernoff started to say something, then stopped. He remembered it was unwise to talk too much about oneself.

"Who will look after this woman when we get her to Malmaison?" Malik asked. "We are not supposed to be nursemaids, are we?"

"I wouldn't mind. She is very beautiful. It could be amusing," Smernoff said. "No, Kovska has given the job to Merna Dorinska."

"That bitch! What's she doing in Paris?" Malik said, stiffening.

"She's often here. It is said Kovska and she ..."

"Who says that?" Malik demanded, a bark in his voice.

Smernoff was never intimidated. He shrugged his broad shoulders.

"Didn't you know? Then you are the only one who doesn't."

"I know. It is better not to talk about it."

"You know I would rather take a goat to bed with me than that woman," Smernoff said.

"Kovska wouldn't know the difference."

The two men burst out laughing, they were still laughing as Smernoff pulled into the courtyard of the Russian Embassy.

John Dorey arrived at the American hospital at 16.40 hours. He was thoroughly irritated because he knew he had lost valuable time, but he had to be certain that the tattoo marks on this woman were genuine. It had first been necessary to locate Nicolas Wolfert, the US Embassy's Chinese expert. It so happened that Wolfert had taken a day off and was fishing on his small estate at Amboise. By the time he had been located, brought by helicopter to Paris, rushed in a car to the Embassy, then put in the picture four valuable hours had been wasted. With Wolfert, Dorey had brought along Joe Dodge, the Embassy's top photographer.

Dr Forrester, a tall, lean man with tired, dark ringed eyes received Dorey in his office while Wolfert and Dodge waited in the corridor.

Forrester had already been alerted by O'Halloran of the possible importance of his patient and was more than willing to co-operate.

"This could be top secret," Dorey said as he sat down. "I'm relying on you, doctor, to see this woman isn't got at. There are plenty of reasons why she should be murdered. I want her food prepared only by someone you can completely trust and no nurse, unless you can guarantee her, is to attend her."

Forrester nodded.

"Captain O'Halloran has already gone over this with me. I'm doing my best. What else do you want?"

"I want photos of the tattoo marks. I have a photographer waiting."

Forrester frowned.

"The marks are on the woman's buttock." He leaned back and surveyed Dorey. "You can't send some strange man into her room, expect her to expose herself while he takes photos. This I can't allow."

"So she's conscious?"

"Of course she is conscious. She's been conscious now for the last three days and she is in a very highly nervous state."

"I must have those photographs," Dorey said, a rasp in his voice. "They may even have to be sent to the President. Give her a shot of Pentathol. Then she won't know she has been photographed. It won't take more than a few minutes. I also want my Chinese expert to see the markings. Let's get it done right away."

Forrester hesitated, then shrugged.

"Well, if it's that important," he said, reached for the telephone, spoke quietly, then hung up. "Your men can go up in ten minutes."

"Fine." Dorey went to the door and spoke to Dodge, then he came back and sat down again. "Tell me about this woman."

"On arrival she was found ..."

"I know all that. I read your report," Dorey said impatiently. "What I want to know is ... is she faking? Is she really suffering from amnesia?"

"I would say so. She doesn't respond to hypnotism. She had on arrival a small bruise at the back of her head. This could have come when she collapsed and it might have caused loss of memory. It is a little rare, but it could be possible. Yes, I think her loss of memory is genuine."

"Any idea how long it could last?"

"Your guess is as good as mine. A week ... a month ... I don't think longer than a month."

"How about scopolamine?"

Forrester smiled.

"We considered using scopolamine, but it is dangerous. If she is faking, it would work, but if she isn't, there's always the risk it would drive her memory deeper into herself. If you want to try it, I won't object, but if she is really suffering from amnesia then scopolamine could retard her memory recovery by months."

Dorey thought for a long moment, then he got to his feet.

"I'll see you again after I've talked to my Chinese expert. Thanks, doc, for your co-operation. I'll try and get her moved as soon as I can organise a place for her."

Thirty minutes later, Wolfert, a squat balding man whose pink and white complexion belied his forty-six years, came into the small room Forrester had put at Dorey's disposal. With Dorey was O'Halloran.

"Well?" Dorey asked, getting to his feet.

"She's Erica Olsen, Kung's mistress," Wolfert said. "I've seen his initials on his various possessions too often to mistake the marks on this woman. This is a very special kind of tattoo ... a special colour, almost impossible to fake."

Dorey looked sharply at this man who was considered to be the top expert in Chinese customs.

"Almost?"

"I suppose a very clever tattoo artist could just fake it, but I doubt it. I'm covering myself." Wolfert's fat face lit up with a knowing smile. "No one can ever be absolutely certain, but I am willing to bet my pension she is Kung's mistress."

Dorey looked at O'Halloran.

"Watch her, Tim. I'll have to alert Washington. I can't do anything without their say-so." He rubbed his forehead as he thought. "More delay, but this could be something big. I'll get back to the Embassy."

"You don't have to worry about her," O'Halloran said. "She'll be right here, safe and sound, when you want her."

But he was not to know that in a few hours Malik would be arriving in Paris. Even when Malik finally arrived, the Divisional Head of MI6 was so furious that his man had been knocked on the head and had lost Malik that he neglected to warn O'Halloran that the most dangerous of Russian agents was now roaming, unwatched around Paris. Had O'Halloran known this, he would have guarded Erica Olsen more closely. But he didn't know. He assumed a patrolling guard, armed with an automatic rifle, was good enough.

But when dealing with Malik, nothing was good enough.

A few minutes after 6 p.m., a delicately built youth walked into Sadu Mitchell's shop. He carried a small suitcase, shabby with metal corners, the kind of suitcase a door-to-door salesman would use. His complexion was unhealthy, the colour and texture of a dead, stale fish and his small, black eyes flicked to right and left with the suspicious restlessness of a man who trusts no one. He could have been twenty-five, even thirty, but was in fact eighteen. His coal-black hair was cropped close and lay over his small head like a skullcap. His movements were as supple and as sinuous as those of a snake.

Jo-Jo Chandy had been born in Marseilles. His father had been a waterside pimp: his mother unknown. When he was ten years old, his father had been killed in a knife fight. This hadn't bothered Jo-Jo. He was glad to be free and he soon made a reasonable living working as a drummer for a Negro prostitute whose sexual technique gained her Jo-Jo's admiration and many clients. When he had saved enough money, he decided Paris would offer many more opportunities for his evil talents. But here, for a time, he found he was mistaken. The police were unsympathetic to pimps and after being arrested and beaten up several times, he gave up and took a job in a Chinese restaurant as a *plongeur*. Here he met a Chinese girl: one of Yet-Sen's agents. She was quick to recognise in this thin, vicious boy a potential and useful weapon. Yet-Sen took charge of him. Jo-Jo received training and money. A year later, he became one of Yet-Sen's most reliable hatchet men.

Completely amoral, with no sense of right or wrong, Jo-Jo existed only for money. There was no task, no matter how dangerous or vicious that he hesitated to undertake providing the final reward was money. Life for him was the spin of the roulette wheel. His philosophy was what you put in you took out, and never mind the risk.

Pearl Kuo, who was completing a sale of jade to a fat American woman wearing an absurd flowered hat and an equally absurd pair of bejewelled spectacles, looked for a brief moment at Jo-Jo as he came into the shop. She knew who he was. His arrival excited her. At last, she thought, Sadu was to take an active part in the Chinese movement:

something she had been waiting for with longing and impatience.

When the American woman had left the shop, Pearl smiled at the waiting Jo-Jo. Her almond-shaped eyes sparkled, and looking at her, Jo-Jo felt a wave of hot lust run through him.

"He is expecting you," she said. "Please ... this way," and she opened a door behind the glass counter.

Jo-Jo continued to stare at her, his little eyes moving over the flowered cheongsam she was wearing that revealed her perfectly proportioned body. Then he walked through the doorway into Sadu's living-room.

During the hours that Sadu had been waiting, he had told Pearl what Yet-Sen had said.

"He expects me to kill this woman," Sadu had said, his pale face glistening with sweat. "This would be murder. What am I to do?"

"You are only to arrange the affair. You don't kill her yourself," Pearl replied soothingly. Her slim fingers touched his face. "This is for China, Sadu, and besides, now it is too late to turn back. You must obey. If you do not, then I must leave you and they will kill you. I know that. But there is no need to speak of that. If they ordered me to do it, I would do it. You should be proud to have been chosen."

Realising his position, Sadu decided to be proud. He hated the Americans. They had harmed him. This was, when one thought about it, not murder, but revenge.

So he received Jo-Jo with arrogant disdain.

"Sit down. I understand you are to kill this woman and I am to see you do your work correctly."

Jo-Jo sat down. He rested the small suitcase on his knees. A faint, but unmistakable smell of dirt came from him which made Sadu grimace.

Sadu went on, now very sure of himself, "First, we have to find out where in the hospital this woman is ... on what floor ... in what room. Once we know that, it should be easy for you. You might have to climb to her room." Pleased with his planning, he regarded Jo-Jo with a patronising smile. "I suppose you can climb?"

Still clutching the suitcase, Jo-Jo asked, "Is this your first job?" His thin lips curved into a sneering smile of amusement. "Don't lean on it. You drive the car ... I'll take care of the details. You will get the credit ... I'll get the money. That way, everyone will be happy."

Sadu stiffened. A flush of fury spread over his face. He moved closer to Jo-Jo, towering over him.

"You don't talk to me like that! I am handling this!" he exploded, his voice choked with rage. "You will do exactly what I tell you ..."

"Sadu ... please." Pearl's soft voice made Sadu jerk around. "I think he should handle it. After all, he has the experience. Please ..."

Jo-Jo looked at her, then he opened the suitcase. From it he took a .25 automatic and a silencer. He screwed the silencer onto the barrel of the gun, then he thrust the gun down the waistband of his trousers. The sight of the gun and Jo-Jo's professional, deliberate movements deflated Sadu's rage. For a long moment he stood hesitating and staring.

"We'll now go to the hospital," Jo-Jo said. Again his eyes moved over Pearl's body, then he looked directly at Sadu. "First, as you have said, we have to find where this woman is to be found. It won't be dark for another three hours so we have plenty of time." He tossed the suitcase into a corner and walked out of the room.

Pearl touched Sadu's arm. "Do what he says. He is a professional. You will gain experience from him."

Sadu hesitated, then controlling his fear, suddenly aware of his utter incompetence, he followed Jo-Jo out onto the busy Rue de Rivoli.

Pearl watched the two men get into Sadu's sports car and drive away. It was too early to close the shop, but she did light a joss stick and she did kneel for a long moment in prayer while the scented smoke swirled around her.

About the time Malik was meeting Smernoff at Le Bourget airport, Dorey received the green light from Washington to go ahead with his plan.

His suggestion had been considered by the Heads of CIA and the FBI. They had been cautious. In its present stage, they felt it wasn't at Presidential level. This woman could be a fake. But they did accept the possibility that this was something to be treated as a top operation. Dorey's Washington boss had said over the satellite telephone connection: "I'm going to leave this to you, John. Anyway, for the primary moves. You can spend what you like ... if it lays an egg, we can always cover the expense somehow. But right at this moment, I would rather not know what you are doing. You go ahead, keep it unofficial, and if the egg produces a chicken, let me know."

Dorey smiled mirthlessly. "You can safely leave it to me, sir," he said and hung up.

But this was the kind of operation Dorey liked. He now had a free hand, money to spend and no one but himself responsible for success or failure. For the past hour he had been thinking and he was now ready to swing into action. The time was 8 p.m. Malik at this time was in the aircraft bringing him from London to Paris. Sadu and Jo-Jo were sitting in Sadu's car outside the American hospital. The woman believed to be Erica Olsen, mistress of China's leading missile and atomic scientist, was still drowsy from the Pentathol shot. The guard, Pfc Willy Jackson, an alert, disciplined soldier without much intelligence, but very quick on the trigger, was walking up and down the hospital corridor, glancing now and then at the closed door behind which Erica Olsen was dozing.

Dorey lifted the telephone receiver and called O'Halloran.

"Tim ... do you remember Mark Girland?"

"Girland? Why, sure, he used to work for Rossland, didn't he?"

"That's the fellow. He's in Paris right now and I want him. He has a studio apartment on Rue des Suisses. I don't give a damn how you get him but get him. I want him here in an hour."

"Just a second, sir, if I remember right, this Girland is a toughie. Suppose he won't come?"

"Girland? Tough? He's not working for me now. I hear he's a street photographer or something. Anyway, pick him up, Tim. Send a couple of good men after him. I want him here within an hour."

He replaced the receiver and leant back in his executive chair. He felt pretty pleased with himself. He felt he was handling this situation with some brilliance.

Mark Girland!

Not many people would have thought of Girland.

He was the man to handle Dorey's problem. Girland was tailor-made for the job.

Dorey frowned. Tailor-made ... if of course he could persuade Girland to do the job.

Marcia Davis had left a plate of chicken sandwiches and a glass of milk on the desk before she had gone home. Now, Dorey, his mind busy as to how he should handle Girland, reached for a sandwich and thoughtfully bit into it.

2

Mark Girland felt depressed. If there was one thing he disliked more than another it was to spend an evening alone in his cheerless one-room apartment which was on the seventh floor of an old, shabby building on Rue des Suisses.

It was raining, his shoes leaked and he was temporarily out of money. He had eight francs and seventy-two centimes in his pocket. It didn't seem possible, he thought ruefully, that three months ago he had had $5000 safely stashed away in a bank.

The trouble with me, he said to himself, trying to make himself comfortable in the canvas deck abortion that served him as an armchair, is that I am a layabout and a wastrel. I had all kinds of ideas how I was going to spend that nest egg. Who would have believed three miserable horses could have put up such a performance? He remembered with regret the afternoon at Longchamps racecourse, when all his money went into the satchel of a grinning bookmaker.

In spite of losing what he had hoped to have been the means to a new career, Girland firmly decided, after the Robert Henry Carey affair, that espionage was strictly for suckers. He had had the satisfaction of telling that old goat, John Dorey, to drop dead.

Regarding him over the tops of his rimless glasses, Dorey had said, "I don't think you are the type of man I can use,

Girland. You are not to be trusted. You always put yourself first and your work a poor second. I can't use a man who thinks of himself first. So you will no longer work for me."

Girland had grinned cheerfully.

"Who in his right mind wants to work for you? When I think of the dirty, smelly little jobs I did for your stooge Rossland – may he rest in peace – and the centimes I got out of it, I should have had my head examined. So I no longer work for you. Goodbye, and drop dead."

But that speech of independence had been made when he was the owner of $5000, not entirely honestly gained, but gained. But in spite of the depressing fact that he was now continually short of money, he still had no regrets that he had parted with the CIA.

For the past two months, he had made a somewhat precarious living as a street photographer. Armed with a Polaroid camera he had spent his days haunting the tourist byways on the look-out for a pretty American tourist on her first visit to Paris, and there were many of them. The photograph once taken, the print produced, he then spent a few minutes persuading the girl to part with a ten franc note. Girland could charm a bird off a tree, and his technique with women had to be seen to be believed. Often, the transaction successfully concluded, the girl, flushed and aroused, would go with him back to his seventh floor apartment.

There were worse ways of making a living, he thought, scowling at the Polaroid camera that lay on the worm eaten refectory table, but not much worse.

This day had been a complete write-off. It had rained steadily, and although Girland had wandered the streets, he had found no suitable subject. The two fat women he did finally photograph in desperation had threatened to call a gendarme when they learned they were expected to part with 20 francs for a rather indifferent photograph.

Girland regarded the big room with its two uncurtained windows that overlooked the roofs, the chimneys and the television aerials of Paris. At the far end of the room was a kitchen sink and an ancient gas cooker. There was a big radio and gramophone against another wall. A wardrobe and a bookcase with American and French paperbacks completed the furnishing.

Girland, lean, tall and dark, wrinkled his nose. What a hole! he thought. What it needs is a coat of paint, a vase of long-stemmed roses and an erotic blonde with a Bardot body, but right now I would settle for the blonde.

He got up and walked to the open window and stared out at the black, glistening roofs. Rain was still falling steadily. In the far distance he saw a flash of lightning. Shrugging, he was moving to the radio in the hope that there was something on he could listen to when the front door bell rang.

He looked at the door, cocking his left eyebrow, then he crossed the room and peered through the tiny peephole at the two men standing in the passage. He recognised the military raincoats and the snap-brimmed hats and he hesitated, his brain suddenly very alert.

Then he relaxed and grinned. Probably an identity card check, he thought. These guys have very little to do with themselves except to be a nuisance. It seemed a long time now since he had had callers from the Central Intelligence Agency. Who knows? Dorey might have had a heart attack. He might even have left him something in his will. He opened the door.

Two massively built men, their faces the colour of old teak and as hard, moved in, riding him back. He recognised one of them, but not the other. The one he recognised was getting on in years. He was probably fifty. His name was Oscar Bruckman and he was one of Captain O'Halloran's strong-arm squad, notorious for his brutality, his courage and his fast, deadly shooting. The other man was younger. He seemed very sure of himself and he balanced himself on the balls of his feet as if ready to throw a quick, damaging punch: a sandy-haired, flat-faced Irishman with freckles and ice-grey eyes.

"Get your coat," Bruckman snapped. "You're wanted."

Girland moved back, relaxed, his arms hanging loosely at his sides, his eyes watchful.

"That's nice to know. Who wants me?" he asked.

The younger man whose name was O'Brien said, "Come on! Come on! Let's go. Who cares what you want to know?"

Girland regarded him, then he looked at Bruckman, then he shrugged. "Well, don't get yourself worked up," he said mildly. "I'll come along."

He walked casually to his wardrobe, took his short white raincoat off the hanger, his hand sliding into the coat pocket, his body hiding the movement, then dropping the coat, he whirled around, a squat, black ammonia gun in his hand. "Don't move!"

The two men froze, glaring at him, their eyes shifted to the gun, well knowing what it was and its effects.

"Okay, okay, Girland, relax," Bruckman said, controlling his temper. "Maybe we were a little rough. Dorey wants you. Come on! Let's quit this fooling. This is an emergency."

Girland smiled at him.

"You know something? I hate your kind. I hate you big, blustering sonsofbitches who shove people around just for the fun of it. Get out! I'll give you ten seconds, and if you're not out by then, you'll get a blast from this gun! You'll go downstairs and wait ten minutes, then you'll come up, nice and polite, and then perhaps I'll listen to you. Now get out!"

O'Brien said, "I'll take your yellow guts apart! I'll ..."

Bruckman's big hand slapped across O'Brien's face, sending him staggering back.

"Shut your trap!" he barked for he knew Girland didn't bluff.

"You still act fast, Oscar," Girland said. "I was just going to give this stupid ape a squirt."

"I know ... I know," Bruckman said and grinned. "They told me you had gone soft. Still the same troubleshooter, huh? Okay, we'll do it all over again, and this time we'll be nice." He shoved O'Brien out of the room and Girland kicked the door shut.

He stood hesitating for a long moment, then he crossed over to the telephone and dialled Dorey's number.

He had a little trouble getting Dorey, then when he did, he said, "This is Girland. What's the idea sending a couple of apes to pick me up? I told you to drop dead. Can't you stay dead?"

"I have a job for you," Dorey said, his voice soft and as smooth as butter. "There's money in it. Don't act hard to get, and besides there's a woman in it too."

Girland thought of his eight francs and seventy-two centimes.

"How much money?"

Dorey knew this wasn't the time for cheeseparing.

"Ten thousand francs," he said promptly.

Girland suppressed a whistle.

"Have you been drinking, Dorey?"

"Get over here and don't be insolent!" Dorey snapped.

"How about the woman ... what's she like?"

"Swedish, young, blonde and beautiful," Dorey said.

"Oh, boy!" Girland laughed. "Sounds right up my alley. You could have yourself a deal."

He hung up, struggled into his raincoat and turning off the light, started down the stairs, three at a time. Halfway down he encountered Bruckman and O'Brien ponderously climbing towards him. He stopped on the third landing and waited for them to join him.

"I've just been talking to your pin-headed boss," Girland said as the two men glared at him. "Seems like I've become a VIP."

O'Brien's small eyes gleamed.

"I've heard about you, Girland," he said. "You're the kind of goddam layabout I don't like. One of these nights, I hope I run into you, then we can have some action."

Girland looked at Bruckman.

"Your little pal sounds pretty tough, Oscar. You look after him. He might get himself hurt."

"Oh, for Pete's sake!" Bruckman growled. "Let's go. We are wasting time."

Girland took a handkerchief from his pocket, made to blow his nose, dropped the handkerchief and bent to pick it up. His movements were so casual the two men merely watched with impatience.

Girland suddenly snatched at O'Brien's trousers cuffs, got a grip and heaved upwards.

O'Brien gave a choked yell as he somersaulted down the stairs. His back crashed against the banister rail, smashed through it and he thudded to the lower floor. A shower of broken woodwork and dust fell on him. He moved weakly, then flopped over on his side.

His eyes popping, Bruckman looked over the broken banister rail, then turned and stared at Girland who was putting his handkerchief in his pocket, his lean, dark face expressionless.

"You crazy bastard!" Bruckman gasped. "You've probably killed him!"

"Not him ... he's tough," Girland said mildly, then with a lightning movement, he grabbed Bruckman's hat brim in both hands and crammed the hat over Bruckman's eyes. As the big man staggered back, cursing, Girland slammed a punch low down into Bruckman's solid belly. Bruckman dropped onto his knees, gasping. Humming happily, Girland started down the stairs, jumped over O'Brien's prostrate body and continued on down to the street.

As he emerged into the rain and crossed to where his dilapidated Fiat 600 was parked, he decided that life, after all wasn't so bad. This was the first time he could remember in months that he had really enjoyed himself.

A number of nurses came hurrying out of the Staff exit of the American hospital and began walking down the broad Boulevard Victor Hugo towards the Nurses' Annexe. Some of them sheltered under umbrellas, others made do with their capes against the fine drizzle that was falling.

Jo-Jo sitting in Sadu's sports car, jerked a dirty thumb towards the group of girls as they passed the car.

"One of them will know which room she's in," he said. "Time's getting on. Ask them."

"Don't be a fool!" Sadu snapped. "Is it likely they would tell me? Besides, we would attract attention."

"Look ... here's one coming on her own. Tell her you're a newspaper man. We've got to know where this bitch is."

Sadu hesitated.

The group of nurses had disappeared into the wet darkness. He saw a girl on her own, wearing a cloak, coming down the boulevard which had suddenly become deserted. He knew what Jo-Jo had said made sense. They couldn't just sit there. Somehow he had to find out where this woman was.

He got out of the car which was parked outside one of the vast apartment blocks that was under construction. The blank, glassless windows made black squares in the face of the white wall, towering above him. The inevitable clutter and mess, the big concrete mixer, the planks of wood and the coils of wire choked up the entrance to what would be before very long more homes for the wealthy of Paris.

The nurse came abreast of him. In the half-darkness he could see she was young and dark.

"Excuse me, mademoiselle," he said with an exaggerated bow. "I am representing *Paris Match*. Could you kindly tell me on what floor and in what room this woman is who has lost her memory?"

The nurse stopped and looked at him.

"Pardon, monsieur?"

"It is of interest to my paper," Sadu said, restraining his impatience with difficulty. "We would like to know on what floor and in what room this woman is ... the woman with the tattoo marks."

The nurse retreated a step.

"I can't tell you that. You must ask at the Information desk," she said. "If they want you to know, they will tell you."

Out of the corner of his eye, Sadu saw Jo-Jo leave the car, moving as swiftly and as silently as an attacking snake. He came up behind the nurse as she was beginning to move away. His right hand flashed up and the nurse gave a choked cry and then fell forward. Instinctively, Sadu grabbed her, holding her against him. He looked wildly down the long dark boulevard. In the far distance he could see two men coming briskly towards them.

"Get her into the building!" Jo-Jo snapped. "Quick!"

Sadu realised it was the only thing to do. He picked up the unconscious girl and ran with her across the sidewalk and into the darkness of the building. He stumbled over the debris scattered on the ground as he reached the inner lobby. Jo-Jo joined him.

"Put her down."

Sadu lowered the girl on a pile of cement sacks.

"You're mad!" he gasped as soon as he could get his breath. "She'll recognise me! What the hell do you think you are doing?"

Jo-Jo knelt beside the girl. He knocked off her white cap, then seizing her by her hair, he began brutally to shake her head.

The girl moaned softly, then her eyes opened. Jo-Jo's dirty hand closed over her mouth, his fingers cruelly pinching her cheeks.

"Make a sound and I will kill you," he whispered viciously. "Now, listen to me. Can you hear me?"

Her eyes round with terror, she looked up at him, squirming away from his smell of dirt.

He released his grip over her mouth.

"Where is this woman? Quick! Where is she?"

The girl gulped, tried to squirm further away and Jo-Jo, with a curse, slapped her face.

"Where is she?"

"Don't touch me! She ... she's on the fifth floor: room 112," the nurse told him, her voice shaking with terror.

"Room 112. Fifth floor. Right?"

"Yes."

"Then why didn't you say so before, you stupid fool?" Jo-Jo said. There was a rapid movement and a flash of steel. The nurse heaved up and then dropped back with a long, whistling sigh.

Jo-Jo stood up.

Sadu had seen the movement and had heard the sigh which sent a chill crawling up his spine. It was too dark to see clearly what had happened, but the sound of the sigh had struck terror into him.

"What have you done?" He grabbed hold of Jo-Jo. "What the hell have you done?"

Jo-Jo jerked away. He leaned forward and wiped the blade of his flick-knife on the nurse's cloak.

"Come on!" he said impatiently. "We now know where she is. Come on! We're wasting time!"

With a shaking hand, Sadu took out his cigarette lighter and flicked on the flame. He leaned forward and stared down at the nurse's dead face. He had only one brief horrifying glimpse before Jo-Jo blew the flame out.

"Come on," Jo-Jo snarled. "They won't find her until tomorrow and then it doesn't matter."

"You've killed her!" Sadu gasped.

"What else did you expect me to do with her? She would have put the finger on you and the flicks would have picked you up and then we would all have been down the drain. Come on ... we're wasting time!"

He walked cautiously out of the building, then headed for the hospital.

"Come in, Girland," Dorey said as Girland appeared in the doorway of his office. "How have you been keeping?"

Girland moved into the big room and closed the door. With a mocking grin, he said, "Why should you care? You must be in one hell of a mess to call on me." He crossed the room and dropped into one of the lounging chairs. "So they finally put your name up in gold. My! My! Washington must be short of talent these days."

"You are an insolent sonofabitch," Dorey said with a thin smile, "but I have to admit you have certain crude talents. These I am prepared to hire." He leaned back in his executive chair and studied Girland. "I have been following your career if you can call it a career. You haven't been doing so well recently, have you? A street photographer is getting pretty near bottom, isn't it?"

Girland helped himself to a cigarette from the silver box on Dorey's desk.

"Oh, I don't know. It's a matter of standards. Guys like you want money, power and ulcers. I take it as it comes. I would rather photograph a pretty woman than have an ulcer."

Dorey shrugged.

"Well, it's your business. Let's find out first if you want to work for me again."

"Work for you?" Girland laughed. "No, I don't, but something was said about ten thousand francs. I am willing to work for anyone for that kind of money."

"You seem to have only two things on your mind: women and money," Dorey said. "I suppose you are built that way, but ..."

"I live the way I like to live and it's no business of yours. What's the job?"

The two men regarded each other. Dorey felt a certain satisfaction as he met Girland's steel hard eyes. After all, he told himself, this man had proved himself brilliantly astute, and also very tough. Dorey was sure he hadn't made a mistake in picking him.

Briefly he explained about Erica Olsen.

"This woman could tell us a lot about Kung," he concluded, "and we want to know about him. There has been a persistent rumour coming out of China that he has developed a new weapon. This may or may not be true, but we must know for certain. We also want to know what makes Kung tick. His mistress is the most likely person to know this."

Girland sank lower in his chair.

"What makes you think she will talk?"

"That will be up to you. From the reports I have on you, you seem to have a way with women. Why else do you imagine I am giving you this job?"

Girland studied the glowing end of his cigarette, then grinned. "I can see the apes you employ couldn't handle this one. You know, Dorey, you are smarter than I thought you were."

"Try not to be insolent," Dorey snapped. "Then you will do this job?"

"I didn't say that. Don't let's rush it. Exactly what am I to do?"

"Her loss of memory appears to be genuine. Her doctor thinks it will return by slow degrees. You are to live with her and to report to me everything she comes out with about Kung."

Girland sat up.

"Live with her? What do you mean?"

"You are to play the role of her husband," Dorey said, resting his elbows on the desk. "At the moment she has no idea who she is, what her background is ... she knows nothing. So you arrive as her husband. She has to accept you. You will have all the necessary proof if she needs convincing. I have your marriage certificate and her passport made out as Mrs Erica Girland. You are a rich businessman on vacation in the South of France. This woman ... your wife ... disappeared while you were in Paris on business. You eventually find her in the American hospital. You naturally take her back to your villa in Eze. There you will help her recover her memory. Sooner or later she will come out with some information, and this is the information I want and I am paying for."

Girland leaned back and shook his head in wonderment. "You certainly get ideas!" he said and his admiration was genuine, "but let's think about this. Suppose she gets her memory back suddenly and all in one piece? I'm going to look an awful dope pretending to be her husband, aren't I?"

"That isn't likely, and if it does happen, you are being paid to look an awful dope," Dorey said smoothly.

Girland laughed.

"What's this about a villa in Eze?"

"It belongs to me," Dorey said, not without some smug satisfaction. "It is isolated, comfortable and safe. My servant will look after you both."

"Well! Well!" Girland looked amazed. "No wonder you risk ulcers. You're doing yourself pretty well, aren't you?"

Dorey shrugged.

"So I take it you will do the job?"

"I'm not completely sold. From what I heard from Rossland, you have never given anything good away. How do I know this Swede isn't fat and ugly? Even for ten thousand francs I wouldn't want to be the husband of an unattractive woman."

"You waste time, Girland," Dorey said and took a glossy photograph from his desk drawer. He flicked it across his desk, knowing it was his trump card. "Here is part of her anatomy, showing the tattoo marks. Perhaps this will assure you that at least she isn't fat."

Girland studied the photograph, his eyes alight with interest. He gave a long, low whistle.

"Wow! Is her top as good as her bottom?"

Dorey passed over a US passport.

"The photograph doesn't do her justice, but it will give you the general idea."

Girland studied the photograph on the forged passport, then he sat back.

"You have yourself a deal. When do I start?"

"Right now. I have arranged a car for you. You will go to the hospital, put her in the car and drive to Eze tonight. You should be there early tomorrow morning. The sooner we get her out of Paris, the safer it will be. This is now your operation. Make sure there are no mistakes."

"What car are you giving me?" Girland asked.

"A 202 Mercedes. It's below in the car pool. Grafton will show you the various gadgets." Dorey passed a folder across the desk. "These are all the papers you need. There is also a marriage certificate among them in your name."

"I'm feeling married already."

"The story broke in *France-Matin*. Watch out ... I imagine the Chinese and probably the Soviets are now interested in this woman. So when I say watch out, I mean watch out."

"I should have known there was a snag." Girland got to his feet. "Wasn't there something said about money?"

Dorey pushed a packet of one hundred franc notes across his desk.

"That's two thousand on account. You'll get the rest when you have some information for me."

Girland stowed the money away in his hip pocket.

"How about expense money? I'll have to buy a complete outfit. You don't expect me to impersonate a rich businessman without the trimmings, do you? I'll want at least ..."

"You won't get it," Dorey said firmly. "Diallo, my servant, will arrange what is necessary for you to have. I have already talked to him on the telephone and I have arranged with my bank for a sum for him to draw on. You don't draw on it, Girland. Understand?"

"Your trust in me is touching," Girland said cheerfully.

Dorey ignored this. He opened a drawer in his desk and took out a small plastic box.

"Here is a gimmick that might be useful." He pushed the box across the desk. "It's a radio pill ... the size of a grape pip. Get this woman to swallow it. If you happen to be unlucky and lose her, with this pill, we can find her again."

"That's neat." Girland picked up the box and opened it. He looked at the tiny black pill. "How does it work?"

"The heat of the body causes the transistor battery to become active. Anyone having a specially tuned radar receiver can pick up the bleeps within a radius of a hundred kilometres. The pill remains active for forty-eight hours. Carry it under your thumbnail and be careful you don't lose it."

As Girland fixed the pill under his thumbnail he said, "So you are expecting trouble?"

"I always expect trouble. Then if it doesn't happen, I'm surprised. It's better than the other way around. You won't be on your own, Girland. My men will be watching you. Your job is to get her to Eze. Don't take any chances. Once you are at Eze, you should be safe."

"Looks as if I'm going to earn my money after all," Girland said ruefully. "Okay, I'll get off. As soon as we arrive, I'll call you."

He left the office and walked to the elevator a little less enthusiastic than when he had arrived.

Pfc Willy Jackson shifted his automatic rifle from one arm to the other to look at his strap watch. The time was 10.10 p.m., and he stifled a sigh. He had more than two more hours of duty before he was relieved. Still, he told himself, it could be a lot worse. Patrolling a hospital corridor was a damned sight better than standing in the rain outside SHAPE Headquarters. It was more than a darn sight better, he decided as a nurse came briskly down the corridor, giving him a friendly smile and passing on, swinging her hips and touching her hair with the practised hand of a woman who knows she is being admired.

Pfc Willy Jackson was a well disciplined soldier who had ambitions. All that talk about every soldier having a Marshal's baton in his knapsack was food and drink to Jackson. He considered Eisenhower, Bradley and Patton the three greatest men who had ever lived. In another twenty years, he also could be a General. Willy Jackson was twenty-three. He was brimful of confidence: one of the best shots in the Army, the champion light heavyweight boxer of his Battalion and the best pitcher of the SHAPE baseball team. Jackson had everything that made an excellent soldier ... and that was to be his downfall.

While he was thinking with some pleasure what he and the nurse who had just passed could do together if ever he had the opportunity of meeting her off duty, the elevator doors opened and a man, dressed in the uniform of an American Staff Colonel, stepped into the corridor.

Willy Jackson was susceptible to rank. A Captain made him tread carefully: a Major brought him out in a sweat: a Colonel reduced him to an inarticulate idiot.

It was his greatest ambition to reach the rank of Colonel when he was thirty years of age, and when he saw this squat, powerfully built man wearing an immaculate uniform with three blazing rows of combat ribbons, his mouth turned dry and he presented arms with a slap and a stamp that shook the corridor.

Smernoff, a little awkward in his brand new uniform, his hand hovering close to the butt of the gun he had on his hip, regarded him. He had already been informed about Jackson. He hoped he would have no trouble with him.

"What are you doing here, soldier?" he barked, coming to rest in front of Jackson.

"Guarding the corridor, sir," Jackson said, sweat breaking out on his freckled face. This was the first time in his military career that an officer of a majority rank had deigned to speak to him.

"Where's General Wainright's room?"

"No. 147, sir."

"You guarding General Wainright?"

"No, sir. This woman in No. 140."

"Oh, yeah." Smernoff relaxed a little. He hadn't thought it would be this easy. "I've read about her. At ease, soldier."

Jackson slightly relaxed. He allowed his blue, somewhat innocent eyes to meet Smernoff's dark, cruel, beady eyes, then he abruptly looked away.

What a man! he thought. Jackson! You have got to get with it! You've got to cultivate the way this guy looks!

"This woman," Smernoff said, hooking his thumbs into his trousers pockets. "Have you seen her?"

"No, sir."

"They say she has Chinese marks tattooed on her arse. Is that right?"

"I wouldn't know, sir."

"How's the General?"

"I wouldn't know, sir."

"Soldier let me tell you something: you're lucky to be a Pfc." Smernoff was beginning to enjoy himself. "You don't have to worry about goddam Generals. What room did you say the old bull was in?"

Jackson flinched. He considered General Robert Wainright was a fine soldier. This disrespect shocked him.

"Room 147, sir."

"Okay, carry on, soldier," and Smernoff began to walk, heavy-footed, erect and very much the Colonel down the corridor. Then he stopped short, turned and cursed.

"You … soldier!"

Jackson stiffened to attention.

"Sir!"

"Go down to my Jeep. I have left my goddamn briefcase!"

Automatically, Jackson turned and started for the elevator, then stopped.

"Excuse me, sir. I am on guard." The agony in his voice nearly made Smernoff laugh.

"You're relieved! I'm here, aren't I? Get my briefcase!"

"Yes, sir."

Jackson pressed the call button and when the elevator doors swished open, he entered the cage and descended to the lobby.

Parked in the drive, in the shadows, was a military Jeep. Jackson ran over to it. Two Pfcs were standing, talking together. They turned as Jackson came up.

"The Colonel's briefcase," Jackson snapped.

"Oh, yeah," one of the soldiers said. Then things happened so fast Jackson later had only a vague idea just what did happen. The nearest soldier hit him on the side of his jaw, his fist encased in a brass knuckle duster. His companion snatched the automatic rifle out of Jackson's hand as he fell. The other soldier dragged the unconscious man into the Jeep, handed his companion a bulky briefcase, threw a tarpaulin over Jackson and drove rapidly away.

Kordak, the remaining soldier, ran back to the hospital. At the entrance, he slowed, nodded to the reception clerk who stared with boredom at him, then entered the elevator and was whisked to the fourth floor.

Smernoff was pacing up and down.

"Well?"

Kordak, a slim, dark, weasel-faced man who had worked with Smernoff for some time, nodded and grinned.

"No trouble at all."

He gave Smernoff the briefcase, then shouldering the automatic rifle, he began to patrol the corridor.

Smernoff went into a nearby lavatory. He took from the briefcase a doctor's white coat which he put on over his uniform. He hid his peaked cap in a laundry basket. Then he took from the briefcase a stethoscope which he hung around his neck and a small flat box which contained a hypodermic and a phial of colourless fluid. His movements were swift, and in a few seconds the American Colonel had changed into a businesslike looking Ward Doctor.

He walked out into the corridor.

Kordak was coming towards him.

"Get a wheel stretcher!" Smernoff snapped. "There must be one on this landing," and he walked quickly down the corridor until he came to a door numbered 140.

He opened the door and walked into a dimly lit room where a woman lay in a hospital bed. Her honey-coloured hair made a frame to her white, beautiful face. Large dark-blue eyes looked sleepily at him as he came up to the bed.

"Good evening," Smernoff said. "It is only your injection. You must get plenty of sleep."

The woman said nothing. Her eyes watched Smernoff's swift expert movements. He had practised again and again with the hypodermic and he handled it with confidence.

As he took her cool wrist between his hot, sweating fingers, the woman shivered.

"It is all right," he said soothingly and stabbed the needle into the sun-tanned flesh.

Like a black fly, Jo-Jo gripped the drainpipe between his knees and inched himself upwards. His clawlike, dirty fingers reached for the ledge above him, gripped and he pulled himself up, shifting his weight from his right foot to his left knee, gripping the pipe higher up and then pulling himself onto the ledge. He paused to take breath. He had now reached the third floor. Below, he could just make out Sadu walking uneasily up and down by his car. He pressed himself against the rain-soaked wall. Immediately below him, a black and white Citroen ambulance had swung into the drive and pulled up. A giant of a man with silver coloured hair and wearing a white overall slid out of the driving seat.

Jo-Jo wasn't interested. He looked up at the next ledge ten feet above his head. Then he began to climb again. He had one bad moment. The pipe was wet and slippery. His fingers and knees gripping the pipe suddenly failed to hold his weight. For a brief, heart-stopping moment, he hovered between life and death. He slid three feet and his body swayed outwards, then he recovered his balance and grinned viciously. Jo-Jo wasn't intimidated by death. That was a hazard he was ready to accept in return for money.

Far below, Sadu watched his progress, saw him nearly fall and drew in a quick hissing breath. He watched the dark figure hoist itself to the fourth floor ledge, pause and then start for the fifth floor.

Rain fell on Sadu's heated face. He was aware of the thumping of his heart. Another group of nurses, busily chattering and laughing, came out of the hospital gates and moved past him. Sadu, afraid of being noticed, got back into his car and lit a cigarette with a shaking hand. He was glad to have an excuse not to watch Jo-Jo's climb as Jo-Jo began to edge along the ledge, peering into the lighted windows while he searched for Erica Olsen.

Jo-Jo wasn't to know that the nurse he had murdered had lied to him and there were no women patients on the fifth floor and no room numbered 112.

He was still creeping along the ledge, cursing to himself when a sleek, black Mercedes pulled up by the hospital's entrance. Girland got out and slammed the door shut. Out of the corner of his eye he saw in the shadows a waiting Citroen ambulance. It meant nothing to him. Hospitals and ambulances went together.

He ran up the steps and entered the lobby.

"Monsieur?" the reception clerk asked, regarding Girland unfavourably. Visitors at this hour were never welcomed.

"Dr Forrester, please," Girland said briskly.

"Dr Forrester is not here. He's gone home."

"I've come to take my wife home," Girland said. "Room 140. You know about her?"

The reception clerk, a balding little man with liver smudges under his eyes, brightened slightly. Who in the hospital hadn't heard about the woman with the tattoo marks?

"The woman who has lost her memory?"

"That's right," Girland said. "Let's have some action. I'm taking her home. Who is in charge of her case?"

The clerk opened a file index, regarded it, then said, "I have a note here ... are you Monsieur Girland?"

"That's correct."

"Oh, yes ... Nurse Roche." He picked up a telephone receiver and spoke into it. "She'll be right down."

Girland resisted the temptation to light a cigarette. He was suddenly aware that he was hungry. All this had been pretty rushed. After leaving Dorey, he had gone to the car pool and listened to the instructions about the car's various gadgets, then had driven to his apartment and collected his shaving kit and a few other things he thought he would need, then had driven to the hospital. There had been no time for a meal. Now he was faced with a 900 kilometre drive with a woman who had lost her memory and could be tricky. It was going to be quite a night, he thought, shaking his head.

A young nurse came from the elevator. She was under twenty years of age. Her bright little face and her pert eyes interested Girland.

"You have come for your wife, Mr Girland?"

"That's the idea."

"Dr Forrester said you were coming. Have you a car?"

"Yes. How is she? Fit to travel?"

"Oh, yes. Dr Forrester is quite satisfied. Yes, she will be fit to travel."

"Okay, then let's go."

As they walked together to the elevator the nurse whose name was Ginny Roche, said, "We are all terribly curious, Mr Girland. Was it your idea that your wife should be tattooed?"

Girland regarded her, his face serious.

"Oh, no. It's an old family custom. You should see her mother."

The girl's eyes widened.

"How awful."

"My wife is pretty proud of her tattoo," Girland said as they got into the elevator. "I have to watch her. She's always trying to show it to people ... gets a little embarrassing."

Ginny looked at him and then laughed.

"Oh, I see ... you're kidding."

Girland smiled at her.

"That's it."

"I expect you are glad you have found her. It must be dreadful to lose one's memory."

"It would suit me," Girland said. "I have so much on my conscience."

The elevator doors swished open and Ginny led Girland across the corridor to Room 140.

She opened the door and Girland, suddenly aware of unexpected tension, walked into the room. He came to an abrupt standstill when he saw a short, thickset man, wearing a white coat bending over the woman in the bed.

"Oh, I'm sorry," Girland said.

The man turned slowly and stared at Girland. His small black eyes shifted from Girland to Ginny who was looking at him, a dismayed expression on her face.

Smernoff quickly recovered his nerve.

"What is it, nurse? Who is this gentleman?"

"I'm sorry, doctor." Ginny was puzzled. She hadn't been working in the hospital for very long, but she thought she knew all the doctors by sight. She had never seen this man before, but her awe of authority made her cautious.

"She's my wife," Girland said, pointing to the woman in the bed. "Dr Forrester said it was okay for me to take her home."

Smernoff moved into the shadows. He dropped the empty hypodermic into his pocket. He regarded Girland. He immediately decided this tall, wiry man must be one of Dorey's agents. This could mean trouble, and there was something about this man that stirred his memory. He felt certain he had seen him before.

"Well, that is all right," he said. "She has had an injection and she won't wake now until tomorrow morning. Come back then, and she will be quite fit to travel."

When you enter a hospital, a doctor becomes some kind of god. The white coat, the stethoscope and the know-all manner makes an impression on most people, and Girland was no exception.

"Excuse me, doctor, but I was told I could move her tonight."

"Well, you can't," Smernoff snapped. "Didn't you hear what I said? She has had an injection. She will be ready to leave tomorrow, but not before."

Girland lifted his shoulders in resignation and began to move to the door when he suddenly noticed this man was wearing khaki trousers below his white coat and his highly polished shoes were of a military cut. His eyes shifted to the hard, flat face. He had a sudden memory of a man with a rifle, shooting at him in a wasteless desert in Senegal.

"Okay, doctor, then I'll be back tomorrow morning," he said mildly, but his brain was working swiftly. He must be mistaken, he was telling himself. The Russian who had tried to kill him in Senegal was dead. He was sure of that.

He opened the door and was confronted by Kordak, pushing a wheel-stretcher before him.

Kordak's automatic rifle lay on the stretcher. With a lightning movement, Kordak snatched up the rifle and levelled it at Girland.

"Don't move!"

Ginny caught her breath in a gasp. Cursing, Smernoff reached her and clapped his hand over her mouth.

"Scream and I'll break your neck!" he snarled.

Girland moved cautiously back, his hands held shoulder high as Kordak came into the room.

There was a brief dramatic pause, then Smernoff released Ginny.

"Make a sound and you'll be sorry," he said, stripping off his white coat. He jerked out his Service revolver from its polished holster. "Get this woman onto the stretcher! You and you!" His gun swung from Girland to Ginny. "Hurry!"

Girland pulled the stretcher into the room and pushed it close to the bed. As he did so, he removed the radio pill from under his thumbnail.

Ginny white-faced, but quite steady, walked around the bed and stripped off the blanket and sheet. The sleeping woman was wearing a hospital nightgown. Girland was too occupied with the situation to admire her beauty. He took her under the armpits, began to lift her, purposely stumbled and half fell on her. In that brief moment as he recovered his balance, he forced the radio pill into the woman's mouth. As he straightened he hoped she would swallow it.

"Watch what you are doing!" Smernoff snarled. "Hurry!"

With Ginny helping, Girland slid the woman's sleeping body onto the stretcher. As they did so, their eyes met. Girland gave her a reassuring wink, but it didn't seem to reassure her.

At this moment, Jo-Jo who had found an unlatched window and had explored all the rooms on the fifth landing, now discovered the nurse he had murdered had lied to him. Cursing, gun in hand, he ran down the stairs to the fourth floor.

3

When Girland had left Dorey's office, Dorey flicked down a switch on his intercom and said, "I'm ready now for Kerman."

As he released the switch, he leaned back in his chair and picked up another of the excellent sandwiches by his side. He ate it slowly, thinking this kind of situation was what he would like to be happening twenty-four hours of the day. The dull routine, the endless files, the official letters bored him, but when he had a free hand, money to spend, good agents and a problem that required shrewd planning, life really came alive.

A tap sounded on the door.

"Come on in," he said and wiped his thin lips on his handkerchief.

Jack Kerman came in.

Dorey regarded this slightly-built man as his most reliable outside agent. There was nothing spectacular about Kerman. Aged thirty-three, with alert humorous eyes and a crew-cut, he made a respectable living running a garage in the Passy district. His partner, a fat cheerful man whose name was Jacques Cordey, had an idea that Kerman was an Agent for the CIA, but neither men ever discussed that possibility, and when Kerman went off periodically, Cordey carried on with the work of the garage and asked no questions. It was a convenient arrangement.

When Dorey was uneasy about the success of an operation, his mind turned automatically to Kerman. He had alerted him to come to the Embassy before Girland had arrived. Kerman had been waiting with his usual placid patience until he was sent for.

"Sit down, Jack," Dorey said amiably. "Want a sandwich?"

Kerman came over to the big desk and lowered his slight frame into the lounging chair. He was wearing an old, well-worn sports coat that he had bought from Simpsons of Piccadilly when last he had been in London, and a pair of shabby, grey slacks. There was nothing showy about Kerman, but when you looked into the alert, rather ugly face and into the steady, dark eyes, you would reverse your opinion that he was just another rather unsuccessful man.

"Not for me, sir, thank you. I've had dinner," he said and waited.

"We have Girland again," Dorey said, "I didn't want to use him but the situation is such I had no option."

Kerman smiled.

"That means trouble, sir."

"I know. I'll put you in the picture." Briefly, Dorey explained about Erica Olsen and the part he wanted Girland to play.

Kerman nodded his approval.

"It could work, sir. Yes ... of course, Girland would be your only choice."

"He's downstairs in the car pool right now and he should be at the American hospital in half an hour. I want you to tail him, Jack. Don't let him spot you. I wouldn't want him to think I don't trust him. It's your job to help him if he runs into trouble." Dorey slid a slip of paper across the desk. "This is a chit for a car. Get something fast. I'll leave that to you. Girland has a radio pill to give to the woman. I hope he does give it to her. If he does, your job will be easy. Pick a car with a radar scanner. Keep in touch with me. We must not lose this woman. I have already warned Girland that the Soviet and Chinese will be after her. It is possible I have moved fast enough to beat them, but I could be kidding myself. You can call on as much help as you may need. Right now I am leaving this to you to handle on your own. O'Halloran's men are too heavy handed for this kind of job, but you may have to call them in. Don't hesitate if you feel you have to. Girland has a 202 Mercedes, black, No. 888. Get over to the hospital as fast as you can." Dorey slid a packet of one hundred francs across the desk. "This should hold you, Jack, but if you want more, let me know. You'll follow him to Eze. Once there, providing you are certain he hasn't been followed, you can safely leave him." Dorey regarded Kerman. "You know what I like about you? You never ask for money. Girland never stops asking for it."

Kerman grinned. He slid the money into his hip pocket.

"I make a living. Girland doesn't, and don't make the mistake, sir, of thinking Girland isn't a good man. In my reckoning, he's the best you've got."

Dorey pulled a wry face.

"I wouldn't go that far, but he's good. The trouble with him is he always thinks of himself first."

"As far as he is concerned, it's a good philosophy."

Dorey laughed.

"Get going, Jack. Let's have some action."

Ten minutes later, as Dorey was locking up his files, preparing to go home the door jerked open and O'Halloran came in. His red, fleshy face was dark with suppressed rage.

"Hello, Tim," Dorey said mildly, recognising the danger signals. "What brings you here?"

"This punk Girland has put one of my best men in hospital!" O'Halloran grated, coming to rest before the big executive desk. "Now, look, sir ..."

"All right, all right, calm down. What is all this?"

O'Halloran drew in a deep breath, took off his peak cap and sat down.

"One of my best men ... he's now in hospital with a broken collar bone and four fractured ribs."

"Who's that?"

"Mike O'Brien."

Dorey looked startled.

"O'Brien? You surprise me. I thought he was your toughest boy. What do you mean? In hospital?"

"Girland threw him down a flight of stairs," O'Halloran said, his face darkening.

"What in God's name made him do that?"

"Well, I guess O'Brien and Bruckman acted a little rough. After all, Girland isn't much, is he? My boys didn't have to treat him like a VIP."

Dorey smiled.

"Doesn't sound as if Girland treated O'Brien as a VIP either."

"But O'Brien will be out of action for a couple of months!" O'Halloran exploded. "I want you to do something about this, sir! I'm not having one of my men treated this way!"

"I know O'Brien," Dorey said quietly. "He is a fighting Mick. I must admit, Tim, this is good news to me. I was worrying that with Girland's lay-off, he had turned soft, but if he can take a toughie like O'Brien and put him in hospital,

I think it is more than obvious I have picked the right man."

O'Halloran cleared his throat, then suddenly grinned.

"Well, he certainly took the starch out of that Irish bastard," he said, "but I must put it on record, sir, that I am objecting."

"I'll make a note of it," Dorey said gravely. "Girland is quite a character. Of course he needs watching, and I think he is thoroughly untrustworthy, but in certain circumstances, he is the best man we have. I have put Kerman on his tail. Kerman may need help. I have told him to call on you if he does. Was there anything else?"

O'Halloran rubbed his jaw, then shrugged. He had made his complaint. There was no point in taking it further. He said, "We have been checking on this woman. We have a report from Peking that Kung's mistress has been missing since June 23rd. A lone woman, matching Erica Olsen's description, travelled by train from Peking to the Hong Kong border. Two days later, she took a plane to Istanbul and stayed two days at the Hilton Hotel. She travelled under the name of Naomi Hill. She arrived in Paris eight days ago. One of the clerks at Orly has seen her photograph and confirms it is the woman. We lost her at Orly and picked her up two days later when she was found unconscious. I'm trying to find out where she stayed in Paris during these two days, but so far I've had no luck. When she was found she had no luggage nor a handbag. Hong Kong says when she arrived from Peking, she had two heavy suitcases with her. So they must be somewhere. I can't get a lead from Orly about her luggage. I'm having all the left luggage lockers checked. We could still come up with her suitcases, and this could be important."

Dorey nodded. His thin face was puzzled.

"She might have stayed with a friend. Seems odd no hotel has reported her missing or finding her luggage."

"Yeah. Well, I'll keep at it." O'Halloran got to his feet. "You are moving her from the hospital?"

"She's being moved right at this moment. I am expecting a call from Kerman to tell me she is safely on her way."

When Dorey finally got the call from Kerman, the call came as a considerable shock.

As Jo-Jo reached the bend in the stairway leading to the fourth floor, he heard voices. He paused abruptly and peered around the bend. He saw a soldier, his back turned to him, an automatic rifle in his hand. The sight of the armed man made Jo-Jo stiffen, and then his lips moved off his uneven yellow teeth in a grin. Well, at least he had found the right floor, he thought, but he wasn't going to tangle with a man with an automatic rifle. He would have to go back to the fifth floor, get out onto the ledge and climb down to the fourth floor. By edging along the lower ledge and by looking into the various windows, he must, sooner or later, find this woman.

Then he heard a man say, "Get the elevator open!"

Again he leaned forward cautiously, and was in time to see a wheeled stretcher on which lay a blonde woman. The stretcher was being pushed by a tall, lean man wearing a shabby suit. He was followed by a man wearing the uniform of an American Colonel, a .45 automatic in his hand. Behind him came a white faced nurse. The scared expression on her young face alerted Jo-Jo too late that something was wrong.

While he was hesitating, the elevator doors swished open and the stretcher was pushed into the cage. In a few seconds, the other members of the party had entered and the door swished shut.

As the elevator sank between the floors, Smernoff said to Girland, "Don't start anything when we get to the lobby. If we have to, we'll start shooting. There could be a massacre down there if you fool around. Just remember that."

Girland shrugged.

"I'm not starting anything ... why should I? You have got her: okay, you keep her."

Smernoff sneered at him.

"Dorey must be a fool to use a weakling like you."

"Why, sure," Girland said. "Who said Dorey was anything but a fool? Just don't get rough. Take her away and leave me alone. Why should I care what happens to her? Dorey isn't paying me that much."

Ginny gasped and stared at Girland who made a face at her.

"And you, baby, you behave too," he said. "This woman isn't your responsibility. Don't risk getting hurt. No one is worth getting hurt for."

The elevator doors opened and the party with the stretcher moved out into the lobby.

The fat reception clerk blinked at them. Kordak had moved close to Ginny who remained by the stretcher. Smernoff said quietly to Girland, "Sign her out. You'll be the first to get it in the back if you start something."

Girland walked across to the reception desk.

"I'm taking my wife home. Do you want me to sign anything?" he said to the clerk.

"Certainly." The clerk gaped at Smernoff and then at Kordak and his automatic rifle. "What is all this?"

"She's a VIP," Girland said smoothly. "The American Army is interested in her."

Puzzled, the clerk gave him a form which Girland completed. Smernoff had moved to his side, his .45 now back in its holster, but Girland was aware of the automatic rifle.

In a few moments the party moved out of the lobby and down the ramp to the waiting Citroen ambulance.

Jack Kerman parked outside the hospital in a 3.8 Jaguar and watched the sleeping woman being loaded into the ambulance. He saw Girland and a young nurse get into the ambulance, followed by a man in a Colonel's uniform.

Aha! trouble, he thought and switched on the radar scanner. As the ambulance began to move down the drive, the scanner warmed up. Then as Kerman started the car's engine, a steady bleep-bleep came from the screen and he relaxed. At least Girland had given the woman the radio pill, he thought. He waited until the ambulance had turned the corner and began racing towards the Pont de Neuilly, then he engaged gear and manoeuvred the car from its parking place.

Sadu had seen the ambulance drive away and thought nothing of it. He was sitting, tense, waiting for Jo-Jo to appear to tell him the woman was dead. He was very uneasy. Nothing he would have liked better than to have driven away and to have left Jo-Jo to find his own way back, but suppose Jo-Jo had been seen? Suppose ...? He grimaced. Lighting yet another cigarette, he looked out into the rain at the lighted entrance of the hospital.

Jo-Jo had returned to the fifth floor. He knew he had failed and he was nervous. Yet-Sen had no patience with failures. This could be dangerous, Jo-Jo thought. His cunning mind was busy as he pressed the call button of the elevator. As he went down to the ground floor, he unscrewed the silencer from the gun and dropped it into his pocket. He shoved the gun down the waistband of his trousers. The cage of the elevator grounded and he darted out of it, moving like a swift black shadow, past the reception clerk and out into the rain. His movements were so fast the reception clerk, dozing at his desk, had only a blurred image of a man passing him and by the time he was sufficiently alert, Jo-Jo was scrambling into Sadu's car.

"Get moving!"

Sadu started the engine and pulled out into the deserted boulevard. He began driving fast towards Place des Ternes.

"What happened?" he asked, his eyes watching the rain-soaked road.

"The nurse lied," Jo-Jo said. "I couldn't find her. She wasn't on the fifth floor." He thought of the stretcher on which the sleeping woman had been wheeled into the elevator. This was something he would keep to himself. "The operation was badly planned. We must begin again tomorrow."

Sadu cursed. He slammed on the brakes and pulled up by the kerb.

"Tomorrow? They told me she was to be dead by tomorrow! We'll go back! You have got to find her!"

Jo-Jo scratched the back of his dirty neck.

"How? I can't look in every room in the hospital. This is your funeral. Tell me where she is and I'll do the job."

Sadu became desperate. This was his first important assignment and unless he succeeded, his status with Yet-Sen and more important with Pearl would be worthless. Besides, remembering what Pearl had said, his own life could be in danger.

"We'll go back," he said, trying to steady his voice. "Somehow we will find her."

Jo-Jo hesitated, then decided he had better tell the truth. There was now no point in going back.

"All right, don't get so worked up. I messed it. They have taken her away. I saw them take her out on a stretcher."

Sadu twisted around in his seat.

"Who took her away?" His voice was shrill.

"The Americans," Jo-Jo said sullenly.

"Why didn't you tell me?"

"Don't shout! I didn't want trouble."

Cursing, Sadu slapped the thin, dirty face with the back of his hand.

"You stinking little rat! We could have followed the ambulance. I saw it go, but didn't know she was inside!"

There was a moment of pause, then as Jo-Jo said nothing, Sadu started the car. He began driving at a reckless speed down the dark, rain swept road.

Jo-Jo wiped his bleeding nose on his sleeve. He resisted the urge to slam his knife into Sadu's body. He said, "Where do you think you are going?"

"Shut up!" Sadu snarled.

Shrugging, Jo-Jo squirmed down in the bucket seat. This was his first failure. He was a little unnerved. His face smarted from the slap Sadu had given him. Well, that was something to be stored away. No one ever hit him without regretting it.

Driving so fast that even Jo-Jo's teeth were set on edge, Sadu arrived at his shop on the Rue de Rivoli in ten minutes.

He unlocked the glass door, motioned Jo-Jo to go ahead, then entered the dark little shop. They went around the counter and entered the living-room.

Pearl Kuo was sitting in an armchair, her small hands resting on her silken knees. She looked expectantly at Sadu as he came in.

"He couldn't find her!" Sadu said, sweat glistening on his face. "Now, the Americans have taken her away. This filthy little rat let them walk out with her and we've lost her! What am I to do?"

Pearl rose to her feet, her eyes opening wide.

"Tell me what happened?" she said to Jo-Jo who glared sullenly at her.

He explained how the nurse had lied and how he had lost time searching the fifth floor of the hospital.

Sadu was horrified that Pearl was quite unmoved when Jo-Jo casually told her he had murdered the nurse.

"How was I to know she was lying?" Jo-Jo concluded. "The operation was badly planned."

"Yes." Pearl turned to Sadu. "You must tell Yet-Sen that the Americans had moved the woman before you arrived at the hospital. Tell him you are trying to locate her, and you will know where she has been taken by tomorrow morning, and you will then complete your mission."

"But how do I find out where she has been taken?" Sadu shouted, wiping his sweating face.

"That I will see to. Tell Yet-Sen I have a contact who will know where she is and I have gone to talk to him."

Sadu stared at her suspiciously.

"Who is this contact?"

"This is something you need not know about, cheri. You must leave this to me." She waved towards the telephone. "Call Yet-Sen. Is your car outside?"

"Yes ... where are you going?"

She went into the bedroom, then came out, struggling into a white plastic mac.

"Where are you going?" Sadu repeated angrily.

"Please telephone Yet-Sen. I won't be long," and she was gone.

To say Girland was startled when he saw Malik standing by the Citroen ambulance would be an understatement, but he quickly recovered his poise.

"Well! If it isn't my old Comrade Malik," he said. "I've had happy thoughts all this time I left you for dead months ago."

Malik eyed him over, his flat green eyes glittering. "I don't die that easily," he said. "Get in, and shut up!"

Girland shrugged, glanced at Kordak who was covering him with the automatic rifle, then climbed into the ambulance.

"You too," Malik said to Ginny.

As she moved to the ambulance, Girland leaned forward, offering her his hand, but she ignored him, getting into the ambulance and refusing his help.

Smernoff got in the driving seat and Kordak beside him. Malik joined Girland in the back of the ambulance. As soon as the double doors had slammed shut, the ambulance took off, racing towards the Pont de Neuilly with its flasher in action and its horn honking its warning.

Girland made himself comfortable. He said to Malik, "Don't tell me you walked out of that hell hole. I really thought I had seen the last of you."

Malik leaned his broad shoulder against the padding of his seat.

"You weren't the only one with a helicopter," he said, "but that's past history." He looked at the sleeping woman. "So you are supposed to be her husband? Where were you planning to take her, Girland?"

"Dorey has a room set up for her at the Embassy," Girland lied. "The idea of course, was for me to give her love and attention in the hope she would eventually talk. What do you intend to do with her, now you have got her?"

"That's my business," Malik said.

Girland regarded him with a humorous, sorrowful smile.

"The trouble with you Russians is you take your jobs too seriously," he said. "What's going to happen to me? You know, Malik, we could do a deal. You haven't my way with women. Suppose I continue to act as her husband and give you her information instead of Dorey? After all, America and Russia have a common enemy in China. I am sure I could get more out of her than you. You just haven't the right touch. It would cost you a little, but that shouldn't worry your people. I'll co-operate with you for thirty thousand francs. What do you say?"

Ginny, listening to this, gasped.

"You are a horrible man!" she exclaimed, glaring at Girland. "How can you say such a thing?"

Girland gave her his charming smile.

"Will you please keep your pretty nose out of this? Who cares what you think?" He looked at Malik. "How about it my Russian comrade? How about a deal?"

Malik regarded him with contempt.

"I would rather trust a rattlesnake than you, Girland. I can handle this woman. I don't need you. What surprises me is that Dorey should use you."

"You're right. It surprises me." Girland laughed. "The trouble with Dorey is he is a romantic. He hasn't learned to distrust anyone. Well, okay, if you're sure we can't make a deal, what's going to happen to me?"

By now the ambulance was racing along the broad Autoroute de l'Ouest.

"In a little while we stop and let you out," Malik said. "You can then return to Dorey and tell him you have failed. But be careful, the next time we meet may not be so pleasant for you. I have no orders to kill you, but if we should meet again, then I could be tempted."

Girland gave an exaggerated shiver.

"I'll keep clear of you, Comrade. I wouldn't want to put temptation in your way. And how about our pretty little nurse?"

Malik glanced at Ginny and shrugged.

"She can get out with you. Just for your information, after we have driven a few miles from the place we leave you, we change cars. You will be wasting your time trying to follow us."

"Why should I follow you?" Girland asked. "I've gone through the motions. I haven't been successful. I have had some money so it is now Dorey's funeral."

Malik drew in a long breath of exasperation. This attitude, this talk coming from an American agent infuriated and baffled him. He had always taken his work seriously and had been ready to sacrifice his life for the Cause. This man ... Malik controlled his exploding temper. He knew about him ... a man who thought only of himself.

But thinking about Girland, as the ambulance roared along the autoroute, Malik felt a slight qualm. How much easier life would be, he thought wistfully, if he had this kind of philosophy of always putting yourself first and always thinking of money. He stared at Girland whose eyes were shut as he lolled in his seat, completely relaxed and humming the latest Beatles' hit.

Then Malik stiffened. Even to think this way was decadent, he reminded himself. Leaning forward, a snap in his voice, he told Smernoff to drive faster.

The time was 10.10 p.m. and Mahler's 2nd Symphony was coming to a blazing end when the shrill, persistent ringing of the front door bell made Nicolas Wolfert start to his feet, his fat, dimpled face showing his irritation.

Wolfert lived in a luxury apartment in Rue Singer: a penthouse that overlooked the old and soot-blackened roofs of Paris. He had bought this three-room apartment with the money he had inherited from his father, Joel Wolfert, who had been a successful merchant, selling American goods to the Chinese people. Joel Wolfert's original idea had been to turn his business over to his son, but he found to his consternation that his son wished to be a scholar. After a longish period which had disappointed the father, Nicolas Wolfert emerged as one of the world's experts on Chinese jade and a rare being who could write, read and speak several Chinese dialects fluently.

His father dead, the fortune he had inherited wisely invested, Wolfert now made an acceptable living attending auctions, writing articles on jade and when necessary working for Dorey when Dorey needed advice on Chinese problems.

Dorey had accepted this short, fat rather unattractive man as his Chinese expert. Wolfert, of course, had been screened by Security, but they had been so dazzled by his talents they hadn't dug as deeply into his private life as they should. What would have worried Dorey had he known was Wolfert's liking for Oriental women. His sexual activities, carefully concealed, would have made Dorey's remaining hairs stand on end.

Wolfert, muttering to himself, turned down his expensive Quad hi-fi set and walked across the priceless Persian carpet he had inherited from his father, down the broad corridor, the walls of which were decorated with priceless Chinese scrolls, also inherited from his father, to open his front door.

The small figure, wrapped in a white plastic mac standing outside the door made his heart give a little jump.

"Why, Pearl ... it is Pearl, isn't it?" He peered at the small, beautiful face. "What are you doing here? You're wet. Come in."

Pearl's red-rouged lips curved into a smile as she moved past him. Puzzled, but excited, Wolfert followed her into the living-room. He hurriedly turned off the hi-fi set, then smiled uncertainly at her.

He had met her some months ago at Chung Wu's restaurant. She had been dining alone, and it seemed to him the obvious thing to do since she had smiled at him, to join her. He had been entranced by her flower-like beauty. She had been startlingly direct. After an excellent meal, she had said quietly, "When I am fortunate enough to meet a man like you, I wish to be held in his arms. I have a room. Shall we go?"

Scarcely believing his good fortune, Wolfert had left with her. They had gone to a small hotel in the Rue Castellane. The man behind the desk had given her a key. There was nothing to pay. Wolfert had seen a slight signal pass between the Vietnamese girl and the clerk but he was too excited to care. This could, he thought, as he followed the small hips up the stairs, be one of his most exciting adventures, and so it turned out to be.

Western women, he thought, as he walked out into the hot narrow street an hour later, exhausted, but satiated, knew nothing of the technique of love. Of course, they imagined they did. Some he had known were quite adept at pleasing a man, but when it came to an explosive fusion of bodies, the Eastern women were supreme.

He had met her three more times, and each time they had gone to the same hotel, then he had decided to make a change. Wolfert prided himself on variety. He ceased to go to Chung Wu's restaurant. He found a Japanese air hostess at Orly whose technique charmed him. Then there was a serious Indian girl student at the Sorbonne, studying classical French ... perhaps not quite so interesting, but at least amusing. Then there was the Thai girl. Even the thought of her made Wolfert wince. Inflicting pain on women nauseated him. This was something he couldn't understand. He had quickly got rid of her, but the experience still slightly shocked him.

Until this moment, he had forgotten Pearl, and he was puzzled, but still confident in his charms to be unworried.

"It is a long time since we have met," he said, watching her slip off her wet mac. "But how did you know I lived here?"

She moved with flowing grace to an armchair and sat on the edge of it. In her black cheongsam with the white silk pants showing, her black hair oiled with a lotus bud behind her ear, she made an entrancing picture.

"I want to know where Erica Olsen is," she said softly.

Wolfert gaped at her. For a moment he didn't think he had heard aright, then sudden alarm flowed through him.

"What do you mean? I – I don't understand."

"The woman in the American hospital. She has been moved," Pearl said, her almond-shaped black eyes glittering at him. "You work for Dorey. My people must know where she is. You must tell me."

Wolfert heaved himself to his feet. His fat face was flushed. He pointed a shaking finger at the door.

"Get out! I won't have you here! Get out at once or I will call the police!"

She stared at him for a long moment, her face expressionless, then she opened her handbag and took out five glossy photographs.

"Please look at these. You may not wish your friends to have them. I could also send them to Mr Dorey. Please look carefully at them."

Wolfert gulped. He snatched the prints from her hand, examined them, turned white and shuddered. What he had never realised before was how disgustingly fat he had become. His nakedness revolted him. The blocked out face of the naked woman with him, he knew would be Pearl.

"I have no time to waste," Pearl said. "I must know where this woman is. Where is she?"

Dropping the prints on the floor with a shudder of disgust, Wolfert said, "I don't know. I know she was at the American hospital. If they have moved her, then I don't know."

"You must find out."

"How can I?" Wolfert's white face was flabby with fear. "Dorey wouldn't tell me. You can see that? Of course, he wouldn't tell me."

"Then you must help me to find out." She took from her handbag a small, flat box. "You will use this. It is a limpet microphone. All you have to do is to fix it under Dorey's desk. We will do the rest. If it isn't in place by tomorrow morning at ten o'clock at the latest, then these pictures will be circulated. I have many copies. You may keep those to remind you how urgent this is."

She got up, slipped into her mac and quietly left the apartment.

Wolfert, his fat body cold, stood motionless, his eyes on the box she had left him.

At the junction of the autoroute leading to Ville d'Avray, Smernoff reduced speed. It was now raining hard again and there was very little traffic.

Malik said, "All right ... now."

Smernoff stopped the ambulance.

"Get out, both of you," Malik said, a snub-nosed automatic appearing in his hand. He waved the barrel first at Ginny and then at Girland.

"Well, thanks for the ride," Girland said and opened the double doors of the ambulance. He paused to regard Malik, "Sure you don't want to do a deal? It would be money well spent."

"Get out!" Malik said angrily.

Ginny had already scrambled out and was standing miserably in the rain. Shrugging, Girland joined her. Malik slammed the doors shut and the ambulance took off again. In a few seconds its red tail lights had disappeared.

"You should be ashamed of yourself!" Ginny exclaimed, her young face indignant and rain-wet. "Do you call yourself a man?"

"My mother thought so otherwise she wouldn't have named me Mark," Girland said lightly. "Damn this rain! Looks as if we are going to have a long walk back."

"But aren't you going to do something? This woman is being kidnapped! You've got to do something!"

"You suggest something," Girland said in a bored voice. He grimaced as rain began to trickle inside his shirt collar. "I'm getting wet."

"Stop a car and follow them!"

"Yes, that's an idea." Girland regarded her with a smile. "Do you think if we caught up with them we could do much? They have an automatic rifle and revolvers."

Ginny seemed as if she was going to hit him.

"Then stop a car and tell the police!" she cried, stamping her foot on the sodden grass.

"All right ... all right. Let's stop a car then."

Girland turned to stare down the long straight autoroute. He saw in the distance, approaching headlights. He began waving. The car roared past, sending a fine spray of rain and mud over him.

"The trouble with the French is they don't care to stop on a dark road," he explained. "But let's try again. Here comes quite a fast job." He moved slightly so that he was well in the centre of the first lane. "If this guy kills me, I hope you will send flowers."

Headlights flashed on and Girland, ready to jump back to safety began to wave. Tyres screamed, the car slid into a skid, came out of it, then came to a stop a few metres beyond where Girland was standing.

"Well, at least he's stopped," Girland said. "I'll talk to him."

He ran towards the car which was now pulling off the road onto the grass verge.

Ginny, her white coat plastered against her by the rain, ran after him.

Jack Kerman leaned out of the car's window and grinned at Girland.

"I was expecting them to drop you. Get in. The bleeps are coming through beautifully."

Girland opened the rear door and bundled the girl into the back seat. Then he ran around the car and got in the front passenger's seat. As Kerman sent the car shooting down the road, Girland leaned forward and examined the radar screen.

"Hey! Take it easy," he said sharply. "They're stopping. They're probably changing cars. We don't want to catch up with them."

Kerman slowed. A car with a blasting horn, snarled past them so he again pulled off the road onto the grass verge.

After another look at the screen, Girland twisted around in his seat and smiled at Kerman.

"Long time no see," he said and gripped Kerman's hand. "So the old fox still has no confidence in me. He has to stick you on my tail."

"Looks as if he had a reason," Kerman said dryly. "You could have lost her."

"That's a fact," Girland said, lighting a cigarette. "Remember Malik who we thought we had left for dead? He's handling this. Believe it or not, he got out of that hell hole the same way as you got me out."

Kerman whistled.

"I'll have to alert Dorey. You sure it is Malik?"

"Come on, Jack, how could anyone mistake that big ape?"

The bleep on the scanner began to move again.

"Suppose you drive while I talk to Dorey?" Kerman said.

Girland jumped out, ran around while Kerman slid into the passenger's seat. In a moment or so Girland had the car moving along the autoroute while Kerman called Dorey on the telephone.

Girland listened to the one-sided conversation and grimaced. When Kerman put down the receiver, Girland said, "I bet the old goat laid an egg."

"He's pretty livid," Kerman returned. "He's holding you responsible. He wants to know if you want help. Do you want me to alert O'Halloran's boys?"

"If he asks that, then he still leaves this to me," Girland said sending the car storming down the rain swept road. "Well, that's a point in my favour. No, tell him I can handle it." He glanced at Kerman. "You coming along?"

"What do you think?"

Girland grinned.

"Okay, then tell him we can handle it."

Kerman spoke to Dorey again. When he hung up, he said, "He doesn't seem to like it. It's my bet he'll turn O'Halloran's toughs loose."

"Well, they have got to find us first," Girland said.

Kerman was now watching the scanning screen. He said suddenly, "Stop! They're coming back! Looks like they are returning to Paris and they are coming like a bomb!"

Girland stood on his brakes, stopped the car, reversed onto the grass as another car snarled by, its horn screaming a protest and in less than seconds, he was driving at a steady sixty kilometres an hour back towards Paris.

"Here they come," Kerman said and moments later a Peugeot Estate Wagon swished past them at well over 120 kilometres an hour. Girland caught a glimpse of Malik's silver head as the car roared past. He slightly accelerated, moving up to seventy-five kilometres an hour. The bleeps from the scanner were very loud.

"Our little friend at the back is strangely quiet," he said to Kerman. "How is she getting on?"

Kerman looked over his shoulder at Ginny who was shivering.

"You all right, Nurse?"

"Yes."

"She's fine," Kerman said to Girland, "but she looks cold."

Girland laughed.

"That's her long standing trouble. She was born cold. She even has doubts that I am a man."

"Oh, I hate you!" Ginny said furiously.

"Careful, baby," Girland said as he again sent the Jaguar surging forward. "It is said hate is cousin to love."

The Peugeot Estate Wagon slowed and drove into the gate guarded driveway of an old château on the main road through Malmaison. As the car pulled up, lights flashed on over the entrance and Merna Dorinska came down the worn steps to the car.

This woman, wearing a man's red shirt tucked into black cotton slacks was slightly under six feet tall. Her age could have been anything from thirty to forty. Her black hair was plastered down over her dome-shaped skull and coiled in a small bun at the back of her thick neck. Her features seemed to have been chiselled out of stone: irregular, hard, flat nosed with paper thin lips. Her big hands and her thick muscular limbs hinted that it had been a toss up whether she emerged from her mother's body either as a boy or as a girl. Merna Dorinska was one of the Soviet's most successful woman agents who, like Malik, had won through to the top by her complete dedication to the Cause, her utter ruthlessness and her needle-sharp intelligence.

Even Malik who hated her treated her with caution.

"Here's your patient," he said as he got out of the ambulance. "She is under sedation. She'll be awake and ready for interrogation by nine or ten tomorrow morning."

"Get her into the house," Merna said. Her voice was hard and masculine. "Have you been followed?"

"Followed? What do you mean?" Malik snarled. Such a question infuriated him. He was convinced that women were inferior to men, but in the past, he had been forced to admit that this particular woman had proved herself superior to most of his men agents, but certainly not superior to himself.

Merna regarded him. Her dark-hooded eyes expressed her dislike for him.

"You are dealing with Dorey," she said coldly. "He should not be underestimated."

"I know who I am dealing with!" Malik said furiously. "Your job is to look after this woman! Don't tell me things I know!"

Smernoff and Kordak carried the sleeping woman on the stretcher into the château.

Merna, by no means intimidated by Malik's manner, said, "Then you had better get rid of this car. It could have been noticed."

Malik resisted the vicious urge to slam his fist into the woman's face.

"This is my operation!" he exploded. "Look after the woman! That's your job!"

Merna stared steadily at him, her face expressionless, then she turned and with long swinging strides, walked up the steps and into the château. Malik, muttering, glared after her. But what she had said made sense, he decided. He must get rid of the car, but he hated her telling him.

Smernoff came down the steps.

"Now ... what?"

"We'll get rid of this car," Malik said. "They can't trace her here. Who, besides, Kordak, is guarding her?"

"Three of my best men. She's safe."

Malik hesitated. He remembered what Merna had said about Dorey. What did she know about Dorey? he asked himself. Dorey was old and a fool. He used men like Girland ... a wastrel and a man always looking for a deal. He decided he could safely return to Paris, report to the Embassy and come back tomorrow morning to make this woman talk.

"All right," he said. "Let's go."

As the Estate Wagon moved down the drive and onto the highway, he said, "Imagine that fool Girland wanted to make a deal ... a deal with me!"

Smernoff grunted. He wondered at the slightly wistful note in Malik's voice and looked sharply at him, then he shrugged.

Neither of them noticed the black Jaguar parked in a row of cars.

Girland nudged Kerman's arm.

"There they go. Now let's walk in and take her out."

4

Dorey surveyed the three telephones on his desk. His thin lips were compressed and his eyes uneasy. He was more than worried. The Russians had beaten him to the punch. He knew he had moved too slowly. As soon as O'Halloran had told him about this woman, he should have taken a chance and got her out of the hospital to somewhere completely safe and inaccessible. This comes, he thought bitterly, of being too cautious. He had stupidly wasted time finding Wolfert to check the tattoo marks. He had again wasted time finding Girland. Now the Russians had her and he thought uneasily of Washington. His first reaction was to call O'Halloran and take the operation out of Girland's hands. Yet he had a strong instinctive feeling that if anyone could pull this chestnut out of the fire it would be Girland.

His hand hovered over the telephone which would put him in direct contact with O'Halloran, then like a gambler who pushes his last chip on the red, he picked up the receiver that was connected to Kerman's Jaguar.

"Jack?"

"Right here, sir," came Kerman's brisk voice.

"I want to talk to Girland."

"Hold it."

There was a pause, then Girland came on the line.

"This is me." The indifferent flippant tone made Dorey

boil with fury.

"You listen to me!" He exploded. "Where are you and what are you doing?"

Girland winked at Kerman and slid further down in the driver's seat.

"I am somewhere outside Paris, and I know what I am doing," he said. "For Pete's sake, Dorey, relax. You gave me this assignment and you're paying me good money – at least I hope you are. I'm going to do the job so what are you getting so worked up about?"

"Girland!" Dorey's voice rose a note. "This could be the most important and vital assignment I have ever given anyone! What are you doing? This could be on Presidential level! You've already lost this woman! What am I going to tell Washington?"

"Who cares about Washington? Just keep your big nose out of this," Girland said. "I'll deliver. Relax," and he replaced the receiver.

He looked at Kerman and shook his head. "He should have been retired years ago! Let's go, Jack. I have to be in Eze by tomorrow morning."

Kerman laughed. It was a pleasure to work with a scatterbrain like Girland.

"You are an irresponsible bastard, aren't you?" he said. "You're not proposing to walk in there and shoot it out with probably a dozen tough Soviets, are you?"

"That's the general idea," Girland said. "You and I can take them. I'll bet there aren't a dozen of them, and who says the Soviets are tough?"

"We can do better than that," Kerman said, sliding aside a panel below the dashboard of the car. "We have a couple of gas guns and gas masks here. When Dorey sets up an operation, he sets it up." He handed Girland a flat heavy gun with an inch wide barrel. "Watch it. There's enough paralysing gas in that gun to put a Battalion out of action."

"It's too easy." Girland took the gas mask Kerman handed to him and fixed it over his eyes and nose. Then he turned and looked at Ginny. "Sit quietly, baby," he said, his voice muffled. "We won't be long, and then you'll have a patient to look after."

Ginny, her small, immature breasts rising and falling with excitement, looked at him with wide eyes. All she could say was, "Please be careful."

"For your sake, I will," Girland said and slid out of the car. Without waiting for Kerman, he ran through the rain, across the highway and into the grounds of the château.

Kerman went after him.

They paused for a moment, side by side, as they looked at the château. A light showed in one of the upper windows.

"That's where she is," Girland said. "I'll go round the back. You come in by the front. Kick a window in. I'll go on ahead. Give me a couple of minutes before you start."

Kerman nodded.

With a wave of his hand, Girland moved silently and swiftly across the rough grass of the lawn. It was dark, but not so dark that he couldn't see where he was going.

The gas mask hampered him and he pushed it up to the top of his head. As he rounded the corner of the château, he came to an abrupt stop and stood motionless.

Just ahead of him, he made out the figure of a man, also motionless. Ten yards separated them. Girland didn't hesitate. Crouching, he rushed at the man who let out a half-strangled shout as Girland's charge swept him off his feet. They went down on the wet grass in a tangled heap of thrashing arms and legs. Girland already had his hands on the man's throat, his thumbs squeezing against the throat arteries. The man heaved and twisted, his fists hammering against Girland's head. The struggle lasted only a few seconds and Girland felt the man suddenly go limp. He retained his grip for a moment or so, then got quickly to his feet. He listened, heard nothing, then moving cautiously, his eyes searching the darkness, he approached the château from the rear.

French windows faced him. He aimed a violent kick at the framework, just below the lock. The glass cascaded into the room and the doors swung open. He heard a distant shout and more crashing of glass, then the bang of a gun. He was across the room and was opening the door when splinters flew from the woodwork and the gun banged again.

Dropping on hands and knees, he threw the door wide open. The gas mask made his breathing difficult and he couldn't see clearly. Lifting the gas gun and pointing it out into the dark hall, he squeezed the trigger.

The gun exploded with a hissing roar and the hall became enveloped in white vapour.

Kordak, gun in hand, was coming silently down the stairs. He walked right into the gas. He gave a strangled gasp, and fell forward, crashing down the rest of the stairs to land on his face on the moth-eaten carpet.

Girland moved out into the hall, then stepping over Kordak's body, he started up the stairs. The gas gun, now empty, was a hindrance and he let it drop. Reaching the head of the stairs, he paused to get his bearings. He wondered how many more men were in the house to guard Erica Olsen. Moving silently, he approached a door to his right, turned the handle and looked cautiously into the room. The gas fumes drifted past him. The white vapour now filled the upper landing. He knew anyone getting a whiff of the gas would be put out of action, but he was still cautious. The room was a bedroom and it was empty.

"Mark?"

It was Kerman calling from below.

"I'm up here."

Kerman came running up the stairs and joined him.

"Seen anyone?" Girland asked.

"Two guys out of action in the front room. Think there are any more?"

"Don't let's take chances. You look in that room, I'll go down to the end room."

Girland moved on, reaching the last door on the landing and opened it. With a water-soaked handkerchief across her nose and mouth, her muscular body pressed against the wall, a gun in her hand, Merna Dorinska waited for him.

As the door swung open, the gas vapours moved in ahead of Girland. Even with the handkerchief offering some protection, the gas began to attack Merna. Before she could prevent it, she coughed. At the sound, Girland darted into the room, swung around and closed with her. Her gun went off, but Girland had already gripped her wrist and the bullet ploughed into the ceiling. He clawed off the handkerchief as Merna's fist slammed against his cheekbone, sending him staggering back. The woman took two unsteady steps towards him, trying to lift the gun. Then the gas overpowered her and she dropped to the floor.

Girland fumbled for the light switch and turned it on as Kerman came to the doorway.

They both looked at Erica Olsen as she lay in the big bed.

"Well, here she is again. Let's get her out of here,"

Girland said. He gathered the unconscious woman off the bed, and holding her close to him, he half-walked, half-ran down the stairs and out into the rain.

Kerman followed him.

They crossed the road and shoved the sleeping woman into the back seat, then Girland tore off his gas mask.

"Let's go," he said, then as he got into the driving seat, he turned to smile at Ginny who was staring, her eyes large and round. "She's your patient now, baby. Look after her."

As Kerman scrambled in beside him, Girland sent the Jaguar roaring towards the South.

Marcia Davis was taking the cover off her IBM 72 electric typewriter when the door pushed open and Nicolas Wolfert came in. The time was 8.55 p.m. The sight of this short, fat balding man at this early hour made Marcia's flesh creep.

"Good morning," Wolfert said. Under his arm, he clutched a bulging briefcase. "I hope I'm not too early. Is Mr Dorey free?"

Marcia knew of Wolfert's reputation for brilliancy and also of his impressive knowledge of China, but there was something about him which she loathed. To her, he was a soft, slimy slug and she knew instinctively as he stood looking at her, his soft, full lips creased in a smile, sweat beads glistening on his bald head, he was mentally taking off her clothes and mentally raping her.

She looked fixedly at him until Wolfert's eyes shifted, then she picked up the telephone receiver.

"Mr Wolfert," she said, when Dorey's voice came over the line.

"Send him in," Dorey said.

She flicked a well-manicured finger towards Dorey's

door.

"Go on ahead."

Wolfert ran his eyes over her body once more, then walked across the small office, tapped on the door, opened it and walked into Dorey's big room.

Before leaving his penthouse, Wolfert had drunk three large brandies. His nerves were so jumpy that he felt he couldn't go through his dangerous assignment without the aid of alcohol. Even now he was in a profuse sweat and every now and then, his fat, wet fingers touched the limpet microphone that Pearl Kuo had given him.

There was no question he wouldn't do what he had been told to do. His life would fall apart if any of his friends saw these awful photographs of his lust. He had little sympathy for America. To his thinking, they had no idea how to handle the Chinese who were, after all, people he had been brought up with and whom he understood. To save himself, he was now prepared to turn traitor.

Dorey regarded him with mild surprise. He had been at his desk since 8 a.m. and he had had a reassuring talk with Girland who was at that moment driving along the Frejus Autoroute, heading for Eze.

Dorey was relieved and satisfied that his gamble had come off. Although Girland was, of course, impossible, he had proved that when the cards were down, he was a man to be relied on.

"Hello, Wolfert. You're early. What is it?"

Dorey had to contact Washington and he had been about to put the call through when Marcia had announced Wolfert. Dorey was itching to tell of his success.

Wolfert came to the desk and lowered his fat, sweating body into the lounging chair.

"I am going down to Amboise so I apologise for this

early call," he said. "As I was passing, I thought you should see some photographs of Kung's jade I have found in my collection. I thought you would be interested. You will see he has been mad enough to deface these pieces with his initials."

He took from his briefcase a batch of glossy prints and passed them across the desk. Dorey took them, scarcely concealing his impatience. His mind was on Washington. He had no interest in Kung's jade.

"I didn't know Kung was a collector."

"Indeed, yes. He has one of the finest collections of jade and jewellery in the world." Wolfert slid the limpet microphone out of his pocket and concealed it in his fat hand. He wished he wasn't sweating so much. The microphone, no larger than a coat button, was difficult to handle.

"Very interesting," Dorey said, flicking through the photographs. "Yes, I see his initials. Extraordinary man."

"Yes, he is." Wolfert let the briefcase slip off his fat knees onto the floor. As he bent to pick it up, he quickly pressed the adhesive back of the microphone to the underledge of Dorey's desk. He picked up the briefcase and sat back, mopping his streaming face with his handkerchief.

Dorey eyed him with disapproval.

"You are out of condition, Wolfert," he said. Then he looked more sharply at the white, strained face. "Are you all right?"

"Yes ... yes. I'm working too hard," Wolfert muttered and got to his feet. "A weekend in the country is what I need ... a little relaxation." He gathered up the photographs and put them into his briefcase. "I thought you would be interested. Perhaps I have taken up too much of your time."

Dorey glanced at his desk clock.

"It's all right, but I am expecting a telephone call. Thanks for coming, Wolfert." He half rose, offered his hand, shook hands and sat down again. "Have a nice weekend."

When Wolfert had gone, Dorey sat for a few moments, staring into space. His shrewd eyes were puzzled. Just why had Wolfert come at this hour like this? he wondered. It wasn't as if he had anything of importance to show Dorey. Extraordinary. Well, perhaps that wasn't true. It was interesting to know that Kung was a collector. He wondered if that fact had been registered in Kung's file. He must ask Marcia, but now he had more important things to do. He picked up the telephone receiver.

"Give me Washington," he said when Marcia answered.

The gendarme who patrolled outside the American Embassy stuck his thumbs in his belt and wandered over to a shabby Renault 8 that was double parked within twenty metres of the Embassy gate.

The driver, a tall, slim man with Chinese eyes was opening the engine cover as the gendarme arrived. In the car was a Vietnamese girl, wearing a cheongsam. Her pale, lovely face was expressionless. The gendarme who was young and observant noticed with some surprise that the girl was wearing a deaf aid.

Sadu watched the gendarme approaching. He was slightly flustered as he gave the gendarme a servile smile.

"I'm afraid I have broken down. I think it is the plugs," he said in his heavily accented French.

The gendarme saluted him.

"You can't stay here, monsieur."

"The plugs have oiled up. In about twenty minutes, they will have dried out," Sadu said.

Pearl suddenly looked at the gendarme and her full lips parted in a smile. She managed to convey such a gaze of admiration that the gendarme was dazzled. With a little smirk, he saluted her.

"Be as quick as you can then, monsieur," he said, saluted again and moved away.

Sadu wiped his sweating face and then leaned into the car's engine.

Pearl, her deaf aid connected to a small but extremely powerful receiving set was listening to Dorey's conversation with Washington. The conversation lasted several minutes, then she took out the ear plug and called softly to Sadu.

"We can go."

He hurriedly closed the engine hood and got into the car. He drove carefully back around the Concorde.

"She is at Dorey's villa at Eze," Pearl said. "You must tell Yet-Sen. We can leave this afternoon."

"We? You must remain here and look after the shop," Sadu said.

"We will close the shop," Pearl said firmly. "We must not make any more mistakes."

Sadu began to protest, then thought better of it. Leaving Pearl to park the car, he went into the shop and called Yet-Sen.

"I envy you," Kerman said as Girland slowed and pulled up outside the Departure Centre of the Nice Airport. "Me back to stuffy Paris, and you with a new wife and sunshine. My! my! some people have all the luck."

"Call it talent," Girland said and grinned. "Well, be seeing you, Jack. Thanks for your help. I'll talk to Dorey as soon as we get to Eze."

The two men shook hands, then Kerman nodded to

Ginny.

"Watch him, nurse: he is not to be trusted," and getting out of the car he walked briskly into the airport.

Girland leaned over the back of his seat and smiled at Ginny who smiled back.

"How she is?"

"As well as can be expected. I would like to get her to bed."

"Won't be long now." Girland looked with interest at the pale sleeping face. "Quite a beauty, isn't she?"

"Yes."

Their eyes met and Girland smiled again.

"I'll get on."

He started the car and began driving towards the Promenade des Anglais.

He had already got Dorey's permission to keep Ginny. This Dorey had arranged with Dr Forrester. Although she was very young, Girland found her attractive. Life ahead seemed full of interest, he thought.

They arrived at Dorey's villa a little after 11 a.m. The road from the airport had been crammed with holiday traffic and fast speed had been impossible.

"This must be it," Girland said as he saw a finger post marked *Villa Hélios* which pointed to a steep, narrow lane, cut into the side of the mountain. He changed down to bottom gear and sent the car slowly up the incline which twisted and climbed through Sea Pines and eventually broadened to a large circular turn-around to the right of which stood massive, iron-studded, wooden gates. The ten foot high stone and ivy-covered walls completely hid the villa. Girland surveyed the gates from the car, impressed and surprised.

"Quite a place," he said as he opened the car door and

got out. "Looks like a fort."

He approached the gates and seeing a bell chain, he tugged it. Almost immediately, a judas window opened and a young, fair-haired man regarded him with searching eyes.

"This villa belong to John Dorey?" Girland asked, now not quite sure if he had come to the right place.

"What of it?" The young man spoke French with a strong American accent.

"The name's Girland. That mean anything to you, sonny?"

"Please identify yourself, Mr Girland."

Then Girland knew he had come to the right place. So Dorey had called in O'Halloran's bright young men, he thought as he produced his driving licence. There was a slight delay, then the big gates swung open.

He was a little startled to see an Army sergeant, an automatic rifle under his arm, come out of a small stone lodge nearby. Chained to a hook in the wall was a savage looking police dog who eyed him balefully.

The sergeant whose name was Pat O'Leary, a massively built man with a red, freckled face, and strong, blunt features, nodded to Girland.

"Drive right in," he said. "We have been expecting you."

Girland grinned at him.

"So Dorey's taking no chances."

"No. We have six men here. You won't have any trouble. Trouble will be our business."

Girland returned to the car and drove it through the gateway.

"You'll find the villa straight ahead," O'Leary said, looking curiously at the sleeping woman, propped up in the back of the car. His eyes shifted to Ginny and he cocked his head on one side with approval. Ginny stared impersonally at him, sniffed and looked away.

Girland drove up the drive, turned a sharp corner and then saw the villa which was built on two levels into the face of the mountain with a big upper, over-hanging terrace. There were window boxes of cascading flowers at every window and the villa was shaded by Sea Pines. It was compact, modern and very deluxe.

"Well! Look at this!" he exclaimed, stopping the car.

A tall, loose-limbed coloured man, Girland guessed would be from Senegal, wearing a white house coat and white cotton trousers, came running down the steps to open the car door.

"Good morning, sir," he said, his black face wreathed in smiles, his splendid white teeth gleaming. "I am Diallo, Mr Dorey's man. You are very welcome, sir. Everything has been prepared for you."

And everything had been prepared.

Two hours later Girland, in shorts and sandals provided by Diallo, lolled on a chaise-longue, the hot sun relaxing him, was talking on the telephone to Dorey.

"Quite a place you have here," he was saying and reached for the glass of Cinzano bitters and soda that stood on the table by his side. "You know, Dorey, you have taste. I'm surprised. I thought you ..."

"All right, Girland!" Dorey snapped. "Cut the comedy. How is she?"

"What do you expect? She was shot full of dope by the Commies and she has had a whiff of your efficient gas. But she'll survive. Give or take three or four days, she should be as good as new or nearly as good."

"Should the doctor see her?"

"The nurse says no."

"I want some action, Girland. Don't just sit there and imagine you are on vacation. You know what I want you to do."

"I know, but I can't do anything so long as she's in this coma, can I?" Girland stretched luxuriously. This, he thought, was certainly the life. He looked at the distant blue sea, the blue sky and the distant Cap Ferrat. "All these boys you have here with guns ... are they part of O'Halloran's outfit?"

"Yes."

"So you don't trust me, Dorey. I'm hurt."

"Malik beat us to the punch and I'm taking damn good care, now we have got her back, he won't do it again," Dorey snapped. "Now, take your job seriously, Girland. You won't get any more money out of me until you turn in some reliable information. And Girland," Dorey's voice became suspicious, "what is this nurse like you have down there?"

"Like ... what do you mean?"

"Is she young?"

"I got it. You're worrying that she might seduce me. That's okay, Dorey, she's around fifty with three double chins. A nice old thing, but not my style." As he replaced the receiver, he looked up to see Ginny standing in the doorway. They looked at each other and burst out laughing.

"You should be ashamed of yourself," Ginny said.

"I am." He regarded her. She looked very out of place in the blazing sunshine in her nurse's uniform. He struggled to his feet. "You can't dress that way in this heat. Get yourself a sun suit. Dorey will pay. Anyway, come to think of it, you haven't anything, have you? I bet you haven't even a lipstick?"

"No, I haven't, but I'll manage," Ginny said, regarding him wistfully. "There are some things I need for her. I have a list here."

"What's your other name, baby?"

She hesitated, then said, "Ginny."

"Fine. Now listen, Ginny, relax. I want you to enjoy this visit as I intend to enjoy it." He raised his voice, "Hey, Diallo!"

A moment later the big coloured man, his face creased in smiles, came hurrying out onto the balcony.

"Yes, sir?"

"I want you to take Nurse Roche into Nice right away. She's got some things to get for our patient. She is also going to buy herself an outfit. Have you any money?"

"Yes, sir. Mr Dorey arranged with the bank I could have money."

"Then you go along to the bank and get a lot of money and let Nurse Roche fix herself up. Right?"

"Anything you say, sir."

Girland smiled at Ginny who was regarding him with round eyes.

"Go ahead, Ginny. I'll watch the patient. Have yourself a ball. You are now the guest of the United States of America."

An elderly woman, wearing a tiny flowered hat, an emerald green dress and a mink stole rattled the door handle of Sadu Mitchell's shop on Rue de Rivoli. The door remained locked. The steel grille drawn over the shop window and the darkness beyond the glass door finally convinced her that the shop was shut. She looked with exasperation at her watch. The time was 10.10 a.m.

Sadu, sitting in the room behind the shop, heard the rattling and he moved uneasily, frowning. He hated to lose a customer, but Yet-Sen, sitting opposite him, his yellow face tight with suppressed rage, Pearl leaning on the back of a chair and Jo-Jo in a corner, nibbling his nails, brought him back to the seriousness of the situation.

"This woman should have been dead by now," Yet-Sen said as the door handle ceased to rattle. "Peking will be displeased. I am displeased."

"She could have been dead last night," Sadu said, "but Dorey moved too quickly for us. How were we to know he would send the woman to the South of France? You will admit we were quick to find that out."

Yet-Sen who knew who had been quick, gave Pearl an approving glance.

"This time there must be no mistake," he said. "You are leaving at once?"

"We are catching the 1.55 p.m. plane to Nice," Sadu said. "We are lucky to get on it."

"You will have a car waiting?"

"I have a Hertz rental laid on."

Yet-Sen turned to Pearl.

"Very soon Dorey will find the microphone. He will eventually suspect Wolfert. Do you need this man any more? If he is arrested, he will talk."

"I don't need him," Pearl said in a cold, flat voice.

"Then that is settled. Let me warn you all, do not make a second mistake. If such a mistake does occur, an example will be made."

He left by the back entrance and getting into a waiting car, he was driven to the Chinese Embassy. He went to his office and picked up the telephone receiver. He spoke in soft Cantonese.

The subject of this conversation over the telephone arrived at his small, but luxurious villa on the Ile d'Or, the garden of which ran down to the banks of the Loire.

Wolfert had driven down in his Mercedes sports coupé a little recklessly as when he had returned to his apartment, he had again drunk three stiff brandies.

During the drive down, it had occurred to him that sooner or later Dorey or one of his staff would discover the limpet microphone. What worried him was the sudden thought that they could find his fingerprints on the instrument.

Sweating and very uneasy, he parked the car in the garage, lifted out his suitcase, then walked across to the villa. He unlocked the front door and entered.

Wolfert employed a woman from the village to keep the place clean, but she only came when he was in Paris. He liked to have the villa to himself over the weekends. It was convenient when a girl or maybe two girls came to share the weekend with him.

Setting down the suitcase, he walked into the big lounge and threw open the French windows. Then he went to the cocktail cabinet and poured himself a large brandy. Although it was approaching lunchtime, he wasn't hungry ... just worried.

He sat down, sipped his drink and again thought about the microphone. Would it be possible, he wondered to get the microphone back? Certainly not until Monday. He would have to think of some excuse to call on Dorey on Monday morning, but that shouldn't be too difficult. He relaxed a little. The brandy was soothing. He would leave for Paris by tomorrow afternoon, he decided. In the meantime what was he to do to pass the time?

There was that girl with the mole on her cheek he had

met the other week at that dreary cellar club. She had given him her telephone number. She might prove amusing. He wondered if she would come down for the weekend. It was worth a try. He finished his drink, got to his feet and walked over to the telephone. As he reached for the receiver, he paused.

From the open French windows he had a view of his short curving drive. Coming up the drive was a shabby Fiat 500 which pulled up outside his front door.

Frowning, puzzled, Wolfert peered through a side window. A girl got out of the car and he immediately eyed her with interest. She was wearing a black close-fitting sweater, skin-tight white capri pants and sandals. Her black hair fell to her shoulders. He couldn't see her face from where he was standing, but his eyes travelled down her long back and the lust in him stirred.

The girl took from the car a shabby hold-all, then walked up to the front door and rang the bell.

Wolfert finished his drink, wiped his sweating hands on his handkerchief and walked to the door. He opened it.

It came as a little shock to see the girl was Chinese, but he was now sufficiently drunk not to be suspicious.

For a Chinese girl, she was extremely attractive, he thought: a little too thin perhaps and the nose a little flat, but his glassy eyes moved over her body. Nothing to complain about there.

He judged rightly that she was a Cantonese and, smiling he said in the dialect, "What do you want here, my pretty?"

"You speak my language?" The black, almond-shaped eyes regarded him expressionlessly, but Wolfert was used to that.

"Certainly. Is there something I can do for you?"

She bent and opened her hold-all. Wolfert's eyes regarded her charming little *derrière* sharply outlined by the stretched pants and he drew in an unsteady breath.

She took from the hold-all a vulgar looking, giant size packet of *Pic-White*, the detergent soap he had seen so often advertised in the press and on television.

"I would like to give you this," the girl said and offered him the packet.

"You are very kind, but I don't need it," Wolfert said. "I never use that sort of thing. What are you doing in France?"

The girl regarded him with her deadpan expression.

"I am trying to make a living. If you don't take it, then I will have more work to do. I have to get rid of all these packets before I get paid."

"That's too bad. Well, come in. Let's talk about it," Wolfert said, opening the door wide.

"No, thank you. I am very busy. I can't come in. Thank you."

"But why not? You can leave all your packets with me. I will throw them away for you. That way, you will get your money quickly."

The girl giggled. Wolfert knowing the Chinese knew she was embarrassed.

"Come along," he said. "Come in. I would like you to tell me about yourself."

She shook her head and pushed the packet into his hand. He had taken it before he could stop himself. Now he was getting a little annoyed.

"Oh come in!" He wasn't used to being refused. "You are not afraid of me, are you? Besides, we could amuse each other." He leered at her. "A little girl like you could use a hundred francs, couldn't you?"

She bent and closed the hold-all. Then picking it up, she regarded him with such cold contempt that Wolfert, clutching the packet of *Pic-White* retreated a step. Then she turned and walked back to her car. She got in and drove away.

Wolfert watched the little car disappear around the bend in the drive. He grimaced. Obviously this wasn't to be his lucky day, he thought. He regarded the packet of detergent and shrugged. Maybe his cleaner could use it. He took it into the kitchen and set it down on the table.

Well, now, he said to himself, this girl from the cellar club.

As he started towards the lounge, the bomb concealed in the detergent packet exploded. It blew out all the windows of the Villa. It also blew Nicolas Wolfert into several messy pieces.

It was sheer bad luck that Jean Redoun, a rabid Communist, who worked as a luggage porter at Orly airport and who was in the pay of the Soviet Embassy should spot Jack Kerman as he came through the Customs barrier after his flight from Nice.

Redoun, a bitter-faced, elderly man, had a good memory. He had spent many hours going through a photograph album at the Soviet Embassy examining photographs of men and women in whom the Soviets were interested. He received a hundred francs for any information he telephoned to the Embassy, whether or not the information was useful. So, having seen Kerman without luggage come briskly through the Customs barrier, and knowing he was a man the Embassy was interested in, he went to the nearest telephone booth and put through his call.

The information was immediately conveyed to Malik.

Smernoff was with him and the two men looked at each other.

"Kerman is Dorey's special agent," Malik said, his thick, strong fingers playing with a Biro pen. "If Dorey hasn't a great deal of confidence in Girland, he would call on Kerman. Kerman has returned from Nice without luggage. That means he could have driven down there with Girland and come back by plane. That makes sense. Girland and the woman could be there. Make inquiries, Boris. This is our only lead."

Smernoff nodded. He left the office. Malik continued to play with the Biro pen.

He was thinking the next time he met Girland, he wouldn't hesitate. This wastrel was proving himself more than a nuisance. He would kill him. How he wished he had done so when he had had him in the ambulance. Well, next time, he would make no mistake.

His mind switched to Dorey. Merna Dorinska had been right. He had underestimated Dorey. Well, that was a mistake he wouldn't repeat.

Dorey would have been flattered if he had known these thoughts. He was at this time reading a routine file, satisfied that he had now taken every precaution of guarding Erica Olsen and still a little irritated with his talk with Girland.

His intercom buzzed.

He flicked down the switch. "What is it?"

"Captain O'Halloran wants you. He's here," Marcia Davis told him.

"Let him in." Dorey flicked up the switch and pushed aside his file.

O'Halloran came in. With him was a tall, lean man who Dorey knew to be O'Halloran's top investigator. His name was Joe Danbridge.

"What's it now?" Dorey asked impatiently.

"You have a bug in here," O'Halloran said. "We have been running a check and we get an affirmative signal from your office."

Dorey stiffened.

"That's impossible. The office is always checked before I arrive. No one has been here. What are you talking about?"

"You've got one," O'Halloran said. "There's no mistake. There's a bug somewhere here."

"Go ahead and find it," Dorey said and moved out of his chair. He knew Danbridge. This man never made a mistake. While the search was in progress, he thought quickly back of his various telephone conversations during the morning. There had only been one of importance: his call to Washington.

It took Danbridge exactly six minutes to locate the limpet microphone.

"Here it is," he said, pointing to the undershelf of the desk.

Dorey bent to stare at the small betrayer, then he straightened. An unwired microphone couldn't function without a powerful receiving set not far away.

"I've already contacted Inspector Dulay," O'Halloran said as if reading Dorey's thoughts. "He's checking. Who has been here this morning?"

"Wolfert, Sam Bentley, and Merl Jackson."

"Wolfert? Bentley and Jackson are out."

"Wolfert has gone down to his place at Amboise," Dorey said. "You handle this, Tim. I must alert Girland. Someone now knows where he is. Not that I'm worrying. They can't get near them. I have six of your men down there and the place is so situated, they can't be got at. Still, I must alert him," and he reached for the telephone.

An hour later, while Sadu Mitchell, Pearl Kuo and Jo-Jo Chandy were driving to Orly airport, Inspector Jean Dulay of the Sûreté together with a young gendarme arrived at Dorey's office.

O'Halloran was still there. Danbridge had confirmed that the fingerprints surrounding the microphone had been Wolfert's. A fast car was racing down to Amboise with two Security officers to make the arrest.

The gendarme, nervous and sweating, under the glaring eyes of his superior, told of the Renault 8 that had broken down near the US Embassy at 9 a.m. that morning.

Dorey became very alert when the gendarme described Sadu Mitchell.

"He had Chinese eyes, sir," the gendarme said. "I thought he was a tourist. There was a woman with him: a Vietnamese I think. She could have been Chinese. She was wearing a deaf aid."

Dorey smiled grimly. They must be the two who had listened in to his conversation with Washington. The deaf aid would be hooked to a receiving set. So now he had not only Malik to worry about, but the Chinese also had taken the field.

"I want those two found," he said to Dulay.

"At least he remembers the number of the car," Dulay said, glaring at the gendarme. "We are checking now."

Twenty minutes later, it was found the car had been hired by Sadu Mitchell, the owner of a boutique on the Rue de Rivoli.

By the time the Nice Police had been alerted, Sadu and his party had passed through the police barrier at Nice Airport and were heading for Eze.

5

"She's beautiful, isn't she?" Ginny said wistfully.

She and Girland were standing side by side by the sleeping woman's bed.

"I guess," Girland said and moved away.

She was certainly beautiful, he thought. It made him a little uneasy that he was to pretend to be her husband. He realised suddenly that he was not looking forward to the moment when she recovered consciousness.

"How is she going?" he asked, looking out of the window.

"All right. Sometime tonight she will wake up," Ginny said. "Her pulse beat is returning to normal. I'd say around two or three in the morning."

Girland moved to the door. Together they went down to the terrace. The sun was beginning to sink below the horizon, turning the sky and the sea a dark, vivid red. Girland was still wearing shorts and sandals, and Ginny, now in a white cotton frock, walked to the balustrade of the terrace and rested her hands on the hot stone. She looked down at the twinkling lights of Eze village, then beyond at the darkening outline of Cap Ferrat.

"I wish I were as beautiful as she is," she said, as if speaking to herself. "I would love to be blonde." She turned, resting her small hips against the balustrade and looked at Girland, "Do you think I would look better if I were a blonde?"

Girland groaned silently.

"Why not buy a blonde wig and then you'll know," he said. Women's problems about their beauty bored him. To him a woman was either beautiful or not. "You look lovely as you are." He looked at his watch. "I must have a word with Sergeant O'Leary. I won't be long."

As he walked down the steps into the garden, Ginny looked after him. His strong muscular shoulders, his straight back, his massive sun tan gave her a little pang. She now discovered she was falling in love with him and this realisation came as a shock to her. She watched him out of sight, then turning abruptly, she hurried into the villa and up to her room.

Girland found O'Leary sitting on a stool outside the lodge. Near him was the black Alsatian dog which stiffened at Girland's approach. Girland walked straight up to the dog and put his hand around the dog's black muzzle.

O'Leary caught his breath sharply and began to get to his feet.

"Hello, chum," Girland said, looking straight into the dog's eyes.

The dog regarded him, then pushed its muzzle deeper into Girland's hands.

"Hell!" O'Leary said, relaxing. "You gave me a fright. I thought you were going to lose your hand. That dog's vicious."

Girland continued to caress the dog.

"I like dogs," he said. "They seem to like me." He gave the dog a final pat and then sat on a rock by O'Leary's side. "Looks like we have the yellow boys as well as the Commies to watch out for."

"Yeah. Let them all come," O'Leary said indifferently. "We can handle them. There was a guy here around a couple of hours back. He wanted to know if this was Lord Beaverbrook's old home. I didn't dig for him. Beaverbrook had a place further down the coast, didn't he?"

"Cap d'Ail. Who was this guy?"

"Search me. A beatnik: dirty, young. I told him to beat it ... he did."

Girland rubbed the side of his nose.

"Look, O'Leary, suppose they threw a bomb at this gate ... they could get in, couldn't they?"

"Sure they could, but it wouldn't get them anywhere. I have two boys at the head of the drive, nicely placed and concealed with machine guns. We can't get taken from behind. All we have to bother about is our front, and by the time they get those gates down, we'll be ready for them."

The two men talked of this and that for half an hour, then Girland got to his feet.

"Maybe I'd better have a gun up there," he said. "If we do have trouble, I'd be happier with a gun."

O'Leary grinned.

"I have just the job for you." He went into the lodge and returned with a .38 automatic and three clips of ammunition.

Back in the villa, Girland put the gun on the undershelf of the terrace table, then stretched out on the chaise longue.

Diallo came onto the terrace.

"Dinner will be ready in half an hour, sir," he said. "Another drink?"

Girland grinned at him. He was thoroughly enjoying this feeling of luxury.

"Why not? A Cinzano Bitters. What are we eating, Diallo?"

"Well, sir, I thought an avocado with crab, then a gigot with a touch of garlic. I have a very fine Pont L'Evêque and a beautiful Brie. Perhaps a citron sorbet to follow."

Girland closed his eyes.

"Hmmmm ... don't tell me, give me."

With now a feeling of complete security, he relaxed. After all, O'Leary had told him that trouble was his business. O'Leary was one of O'Halloran's bright, Irish fighters. Girland told himself he now had nothing to worry about until Erica Olsen recovered consciousness, and that would be some hours ahead. He dozed.

"Hey!"

The blonde girl, wearing a flame-red sleeveless dress, who stood before him brought him upright.

He stared, then grinned.

"Well! For a moment you had me fooled."

Ginny looked anxiously at him.

"Do you like it? It took a whole bottle of peroxide."

Girland regarded her small, immature figure, her bright, expectant eyes, her young alert face and he smiled.

"Ginny ... you look gorgeous. Yes, of course, I think you look more beautiful blonde. Come and sit down. Tell me the story of your life."

She regarded him, an exasperated expression in her eyes.

"I don't want to tell you the story of my life ... it is far too dull. Tell me the story of your life." She came and sat by his side, self-consciously touching her hair. "Are you sure you like me better this way?"

Girland crossed his long legs and lit a cigarette.

"How old are you, Ginny?"

She stiffened.

"What's that to you?"

"Eighteen?"

"Of course not! I'm nineteen!"

Girland put his hand over hers.

"I'm nearly twice your age." He shook his head. "I envy you, Ginny. It's wonderful to be as young as you are."

"I don't know what you are talking about! Do you like me blonde?"

"I like you anyway. How is the patient?"

Ginny moved impatiently.

"She's all right. You are far more interested in her than you are in me!"

"Ginny dear," Girland said, keeping his face straight, "she is my wife."

"You don't expect me to believe that! I know all about it. She is no more your wife than I am!"

Girland flicked ash off his cigarette.

"Can you guess what we are having for dinner?"

She stared at him, then stood up and walked slowly over to the balustrade. He watched her, then grimaced. Complications, he thought. She is a sweet kid, but ...

He remained where he was, smoking and staring up at the stars as they began to appear in the darkening sky.

He was relieved when Diallo announced that dinner was served.

Sadu Mitchell was always being startled by Pearl's unexpected knowledge and her odd contacts. When they left Nice Airport in the 404 that Hertz Rental had ready for them, she directed him through Nice, along the Corniche to Villefranche Pass and to a tiny hotel, set back against the mountain where a small, elderly woman came out to greet them. This woman, in a white sweater and black slacks, was Vietnamese.

Slightly bewildered, Sadu watched the two women greet each other while Jo-Jo sat in the back of the car, sneering to himself.

The woman, Ruby Kuo, turned out to be Pearl's aunt. She also owned the hotel. There was a little delay before the three were given rooms as Pearl and Ruby had much to say to each other. Eventually, Sadu got Pearl to himself. Jo-Jo joined them. It was decided that Jo-Jo should go immediately to Dorey's villa and explore the ground. It was Pearl who gave him the Beaverbrook excuse.

A couple of hours later, Jo-Jo returned. He found Sadu and Pearl waiting for him in the small garden that Ruby kept for her own use.

"The Army's there," Jo-Jo said, shrugging. "I haven't a hope in hell of getting at her." He sat down and began to pick his nose. "You are supposed to be the brains of this outfit ... you fix it."

Pearl and Sadu looked at each other. Then Pearl said, "I will talk to Ruby," and she went into the hotel.

Sadu questioned Jo-Jo about the position of the villa.

"It's built against the mountain," Jo-Jo said. "There are high walls around it and the Army's there. There's a police dog too. You can't even see the villa from the gate. If she stays holed up there, we'll never get at her."

Sadu got to his feet and walked to the end of the garden. He thought of what Yet-Sen had said: if there is another mistake, an example will be made. What did that mean? His hands turned clammy. He was now regretting getting mixed up with Yet-Sen. It was Pearl's fault. She had nagged at him, and at that time, it had seemed not only safe and simple, but the right thing to do.

Twenty minutes later, Pearl returned. The two men looked expectantly at her.

"It can be done," she said. "My aunt knows the villa. She has lived here for many years. There is a little known footpath from the Grande Corniche that leads down to the back of the villa. The path is never used now. We could get near the villa by this path."

"Suppose they know about it?" Sadu said uneasily. "Suppose there is a man and a dog there, waiting for us?"

Pearl shrugged indifferently.

"A man and a dog does not make an impossibility," she said. "Jo-Jo has a gun and a silencer."

Sadu regarded her flower-like, expressionless face. He wiped the sweat from his forehead. This woman, he thought, was too dedicated. He began to hate her.

Jo-Jo got to his feet.

"Let's go," he said. "Time's getting on."

"I will drive the car," Pearl said. "You must go with him." This to Sadu. "I will leave you at the footpath and then go on to La Turbie. I will wait there half an hour, then come back. By then you should have been able to see what can be done."

"When you two have finished making plans," Sadu said angrily, "let me remind you I am in charge of this operation. We will not go now. At this hour the Corniche will be crammed with cars. We will wait until the traffic thins out." He looked at his gold Omega. The time was 2.15 p.m. "We will not leave here until midnight."

Pearl and Jo-Jo exchanged glances, then Jo-Jo shrugged.

"Don't we get any food here?" he asked. "I'm hungry."

"She's awake," Ginny said as she came out onto the terrace.

Girland was lying on the chaise-longue. The time was 9.30 p.m. He had had an excellent dinner and was now watching a satellite jinking across the star-laden sky.

He raised his head, then swung his legs off the chaise-longue.

"Do you want me to do anything?"

"She wants to know where she is. I think you had better ..."

Girland hurriedly pulled on a sweatshirt and followed Ginny into the villa. There was a table lamp in the woman's bedroom which cast shadows. He crossed to the bed.

Erica Olsen looked up at him and Girland drew in a long, slow breath. He had thought her beautiful in sleep, but now the big, violet coloured eyes were open, bringing life to her face, she was even more beautiful.

"Where am I?" she asked, looking up at him. "Who are you?"

"I am Mark, your husband, darling," he said gently. "You are home. It's all right. There's nothing to worry about."

"Home?" Her long cool fingers moved over the back of his hand. "I can't remember anything. You are my husband?"

"Yes, darling. Don't you remember me?"

She closed her eyes. For a brief moment, she remained still, then she said, "It is beautiful and black like a grape."

Girland looked searchingly at her.

"What is? What do you mean?" he asked, sensing that what she had just said was important. "What is beautiful and black like a grape?"

"Did I say that?" She opened her eyes. "I don't know why I said it. Who did you say you were?"

"Your husband ... Mark."

"You can't imagine how it feels to remember nothing. I didn't know I was married. I don't remember ever seeing you before."

"There's nothing to worry about. The doctor says your memory will come back in time. Just don't worry. You are home now and I am here to look after you."

"You are very kind." She sighed and closed her eyes. "I feel so tired. I – I thought at one time I was in hospital."

"So you were, but I have brought you home."

"It's a nice room." Her eyes opened and she looked fixedly at him. "Mark? Is that your name?"

"That's right. You try to sleep. Tomorrow, you'll feel better. I'll be right here, Erica. You have nothing to worry about."

"Erica? Is that my name?"

"Of course, darling."

"I didn't know." Again the dark blue eyes regarded him. "And you really are my husband?"

"Yes."

She seemed to relax and she closed her eyes.

"Oh, it's good to be home."

When he was sure she was sleeping, he gently disengaged his hand from hers and stood up.

Ginny and he moved away from the bed.

"What was all that about a black grape?" Girland asked. "What did she mean?"

"I don't know. I'm going to stay with her." Ginny was now the efficient nurse. "She'll probably sleep all night." She looked at him unhappily. "You were very convincing. If I hadn't known, I would really have thought you were her husband."

Girland made a movement of irritation. He didn't feel very proud of himself. "You don't imagine I like this, do you? This is a job. I get paid for it."

He left the room and went down to the terrace.

Kovski came into the small office where Malik was sitting behind a desk, digging holes in the desk blotter with a paper knife.

Kovski was the head of the Paris division of Soviet Security. He was a short fat man with a chin beard, an enormous bald dome of a head, ferrety eyes and a thick nose. He was shabbily dressed, and there were food stains on his coat lapels. He was one of the most dangerous and cunning members of the Secret Police and Malik's boss.

Malik looked up and regarded him with his green snake's eyes. He didn't bother to move. Malik was very sure of himself. Kovski could be replaced tomorrow, but Malik knew his own position was unassailable unless he made a mistake, and Malik never made mistakes.

"What is happening?" Kovski demanded, coming to rest before the desk.

"I am waiting," Malik said and began digging the paper knife into the blotter again.

"We can no longer wait," Kovski snapped and threw a cable onto the blotter.

Malik read the cable, then pushed it back across the desk. He got to his feet, towering over Kovski.

"Why didn't they say so before?"

"Information has just been received that Kung has invented a new weapon," Kovski said. "It is now vital that we should know about it. It is possible this woman knows something. We need the information immediately. Where is this woman?"

"We have one small lead that could mean something." Malik went on to tell Kovski about Kerman. "We are checking. We have four men in Nice, but this could take time. Why wasn't I told this was immediate?"

Kovski drew in a sharp breath. When dealing with Malik, he found no one but Malik could ever be in the right.

"You know now! This woman must be found! After all, you lost her."

Malik regarded him.

"I didn't lose her. Your mistress, Merna Dorinska lost her."

Kovski flinched and blood rushed into his face.

"Don't call that woman my mistress!"

"I am sorry. I mean your whore," Malik said.

The two men stared at each other. Kovski's eyes were the first to shift.

"What are we going to do?" he asked in a milder tone.

Malik returned to his chair and sat down.

"Dorey has a secretary. Her name is Marcia Davis," he said, picking up the paper knife. "She will know where this woman is. I would have done this before had I known it was so urgent. You can leave it to me."

"Done what?" Kovski asked, staring uneasily at Malik.

"It would be better if you left this to me," Malik said. "I am in charge of the operation. I suggest the less you know about it until I have definite information, the better for both of us."

Kovski hesitated. "What are you going to do with this woman, Marcia Davis?"

"Do you want to know?" The glittering green eyes made Kovski very uneasy.

"I hope you know what you are doing, Malik."

"Oh, yes, I know what I am doing. We are wasting time. You either allow me to handle this my way or I must withdraw."

Kovski shifted his weight from one foot to the other.

"We must not fail."

"Who said anything about failing?"

Kovski nodded, then turning, he went out of the office.

Malik reached for the telephone.

"Send Smernoff to me at once," he told the inquiring voice.

He replaced the receiver and picked up the paper knife. Slowly and viciously, he again began to dig holes in the blotter.

Slightly out of breath, and sweating, Sadu paused.

"Wait!" he said curtly to Jo-Jo who was moving down the steep path, gun in hand, his eyes probing the starlit darkness.

Jo-Jo paused and looked over his shoulder.

"What is it?" he whispered.

"You are moving too fast," Sadu said, his voice low. "This is dangerous. We could start a landslide."

The path that Ruby had told Pearl about did exist. It was overgrown with clumps of dried grass, weeds and roots of trees. No one appeared to have used it for years. They were halfway down and from where he stood, Sadu could already see, outlined against the mountain, the roof of the villa.

The two men again began a more cautious descent.

Sadu was careful to let Jo-Jo go on well ahead. He had no wish to encounter a police dog. Jo-Jo was paid for this kind of work: he wasn't.

They covered a few more metres of rough ground, then Jo-Jo came to a stop. After making sure there was no immediate danger, Sadu joined him.

The two men could now look down on the terrace of the villa, some thirty metres below them. They could see Girland lying on the chaise-longue, sharply outlined under the lights of the terrace against the white paving stones.

Jo-Jo surveyed the scene with an expert eye.

"If she comes out on the terrace, she will be a sitting duck," he said. "I will have to have a rifle with a telescopic sight. I'll have only one shot to do the job with. If I am to get away, I'll also want a silencer. A .22 rifle will do. With a telescopic sight, a head shot will do the trick."

Sadu grimaced.

"I'll arrange it," he said. "There is plenty of cover here. As soon as I get the rifle, you will come here and wait."

Jo-Jo picked at a sore on the back of his hand.

"Just so long as she comes out on the terrace," he said.

Flanked on either side by Harry Whitelaw and the owner of the restaurant, Claude Terrail, Marcia Davis walked out of the elegant room with its superb view of Notre Dame.

Dining at *La Tour d'Argent* was always an experience, she thought. The meal had been more than excellent. The *filet de sole cardinal* and the *Soufflé Valtesse* had been beyond reproach.

Harry Whitelaw of the *New York Post* had been amusing, and his attentions, as always, flattering. She had known Whitelaw off and on for a number of years. He was a tall, humorous man with no complications. Marcia was always able to relax in his company. She had never had any trouble with him. He came to Paris three times a year, and each time he took her to *La Tour d'Argent* which he claimed to be the best restaurant in Paris.

Claude Terrail, tall and aristocratic-looking, shook hands at the tiny elevator, then Marcia and Whitelaw descended to the street level.

"That was a perfect meal, Harry," Marcia said as she collected her mink stole from the woman attendant. "Thanks a million. When will you be in Paris again?"

Whitelaw pushed three francs into the woman's hand. He was never quite sure, even after innumerable visits to the French capital, just how much he should tip.

"I'll be over for Christmas." He regarded her as the doorman went in search of a taxi. "How's Dorey?"

"He's fine."

"You know, we have wondered about him. We thought he was through."

Marcia laughed.

"Who didn't? No one should ever underestimate Dorey."

Whitelaw said as casually as he could, "Anything exciting happening?"

"Oh, Harry!" Marcia gave him an old-fashioned look. "Just when I was thinking this lovely dinner had no strings."

Whitelaw grinned.

"No harm in trying. Okay, forget it." He moved a step away from her and regarded her affectionately. "You know, Marcia, you are a very attractive woman. Tell me something: just why haven't you married?"

Marcia stroked the fur of her stole. Her smile was a little rueful.

"Here's your taxi, Harry. Thanks, and I'll be waiting for a call from you ... Christmas."

"You'll get it. You know something? I've begun to ask myself why the hell I haven't married."

When he had driven away in the taxi, Marcia walked to where she had parked her Mini-Cooper on the Ponte de la Tournelle. She unlocked the car door and slid into the driving seat. For a moment or so, she stared through the dusty windshield. Did Harry mean anything by that last remark, she wondered. She was now thirty-five. She was getting bored being Dorey's slave. Although she loved Paris, how much nicer it would be to have her own home in New York.

Don't jump to conclusions, girl, she said, shrugging, then thumbing the starter, she drove rapidly to her three-roomed apartment on the Rue de la Tour.

Humming under her breath, she parked her little car, walked briskly through the dark courtyard, pressed the door release, then entered the lobby. She rode up in the elevator to the third floor. Leaving the elevator, she took from her bag her front door key and inserted it into the lock. She had some trouble opening the door, and this puzzled her. Up to this moment, the lock had worked efficiently. But by pulling the door towards her and putting pressure on the key, she managed to get the door open.

This was something she must look at tomorrow morning, she thought, but right now, she wanted her bed. There was nothing nicer than to have a first-class meal and good company, then come back, throw off your clothes and get into bed with a good book. She would read for twenty minutes, then turn out the light.

She snapped on the lights and walked into her living-room. Then she stopped short, her blood turning cold, her mouth opening to scream.

The chill of cold steel touched her throat as Smernoff snarled, "One sound out of you, you bitch, and I will cut your throat."

Malik lounged in her favourite armchair. A Russian cigarette burned between his thick fingers and his silver-coloured hair made a sharp contrast against the wine-coloured chair back.

"Don't be foolish," he said in his bad French. "All right, Boris, let her alone."

Marcia recognised Malik. She had seen his photograph often enough in the various files she handled daily. She knew him to be the most dangerous of the Russian agents. Her heart quailed as Smernoff gave her a hard shove towards Malik.

"Sit down, Miss Davis," Malik said politely. "We have no time to waste. I must know where Erica Olsen is. Please tell me."

It said much for Marcia's courage and self-control that by the time she had sat down and was facing Malik, she had recovered from the shock of finding these two men in her apartment, and she had also recovered her composure. She knew she was in deadly danger. She knew these two men would get the information they wanted from her unless she outwitted them. Her mind worked swiftly. She remembered Girland had already told Malik that Erica Olsen was to go to the American Embassy. This, she decided, must be her story. It would be hard to disprove, and she must be careful to convey to these two that she was giving the information reluctantly.

"You are Malik, aren't you?" she said, looking steadily at the silver-haired giant.

"Never mind who I am. Where is Erica Olsen?"

"Where you can't possibly get at her."

"Miss Davis, I dislike being disagreeable to women," Malik said, flicking ash on the carpet. "My companion has no such compunctions. You are wasting my time which is valuable. I am going to ask you again, and then if I don't get a satisfactory answer, I will allow my companion to take over the interrogation. Where is Erica Olsen?"

Marcia appeared to hesitate. She shrank back in the chair. Her hands moved to her throat and her eyes became wide.

"I told you ... where you can't possibly get at her. She's in the Embassy."

"I was expecting you to say that," Malik said. "My information is that she is on the Côte d'Azure. Where is Erica Olsen, please?"

Marcia stared into the expressionless eyes and she knew she had lost her gamble.

"Go to hell!" she said quietly, then starting up, she groped for the glass ashtray on a nearby occasional table with the intention of throwing it through the closed window.

She felt a blinding pain on the side of her neck, then she felt herself falling.

Smernoff who had chopped her with the side of his hand, caught hold of her and pulled her back into the chair.

Malik stubbed out his cigarette and lit another.

"Go ahead," he said, and began to look around the room. He thought how comfortable it was and how he would like to own it. Everything was in good taste. There were several good etchings on the walls. One by Springer, a movement of birds, particularly pleased him. These Americans certainly knew how to live well. He thought of his own one-roomed home in Moscow, and he wrinkled his nose.

Smernoff had taken a hypodermic from his pocket. He stabbed a heavy dose of scopolamine into a vein on Marcia's arm.

A half an hour later, Marcia was talking sleepily.

"Dorey has a villa in Eze," she told Malik. "Erica Olsen is there with Girland. There are six of O'Halloran's men guarding the villa."

"How is the villa called?" Malik asked quietly.

"Villa Hélios."

Malik moved away from her and looked at Smernoff.

"I think that covers it."

Smernoff nodded.

"Well, all right." Malik collected five butts of his Russian cigarettes from the ashtray and put them in a matchbox. "Then she's yours. It is a pity. She's attractive, isn't she?"

Smernoff shrugged. Women bored him.

"All cats are grey in the dark," he said indifferently. "What is one woman less in the world?"

"Be careful." Malik moved to the door. "Give me five minutes."

Smernoff smiled.

"You don't have to tell me. I know my job."

Malik nodded and left the apartment. He rode down in the elevator. The time was now 11.50 p.m. The concierge was in bed. No one saw him as he let himself out, crossed the Street to where his car was parked. He got in and drove away.

Alone in the apartment, Smernoff helped Marcia to her feet.

"You need some fresh air," he said and led her willingly to the open French window and out onto the balcony. He stood by her side looking down at the Rue de la Tour. At this hour, the street was deserted.

Marcia, drugged, sleepy and relaxed, put her hands on the damp balcony rail and breathed in the close night air.

Smernoff looked up and down the street. He looked intently at the lighted windows of the various nearby apartment. No one was out on their balconies. He stepped behind Marcia, bent, gripped her ankles tightly and heaved upwards.

She fell soundlessly, breaking her neck, her back and her right arm as she landed on the top of a parked Dauphine.

Ginny came out onto the terrace. Girland lifted his head and laid down the paperback he was reading.

"Well? How is she?"

"She's all right," Ginny said and sat in a chair near him. "She's sleeping. I've given her a mild sedative. She should be able to get up tomorrow." She looked at him. "Then you will have to play your role as her husband."

Girland shrugged.

"I told you ... it's a job. I get paid for it."

"I don't think I want to stay here," Ginny said, looking down at her hands. "I would rather return to the hospital."

"This is your job, Ginny," Girland reminded her. "You're getting paid for it too."

"She won't need a nurse after tomorrow."

"Okay, then let's wait until tomorrow before you decide to rush off."

Ginny got up and wandered to the balustrade. She remained still, looking down at the distant lights, then finally, she turned and looked at Girland who was staring up at the stars.

"I'm going to bed. She'll sleep. Good night."

Girland felt the tension in her, but he resisted the temptation to go to her. She was too young, he thought irritably. I can't afford complications.

"Okay, Ginny," he said casually. "Good night."

She went into the villa.

He lit a cigarette and picked up the paperback, but he found he couldn't be bothered with it. He threw it aside, got to his feet and looked around him. Somewhere in the garden, he could hear O'Halloran's men talking in subdued voices.

"Is there anything else, sir?" Diallo asked as he came out onto the terrace. "A drink, perhaps?"

"No ... fine, thanks. You go to bed. I'm just turning in," Girland said.

"Then I will sir. Good night."

When the Senegalese had gone, Girland flicked his half smoked cigarette into the darkness, then turning off the terrace light, he walked into the villa. As he was about to climb the stairs, the telephone bell began to ring. He went into the big living-room and picked up the receiver.

It was Dorey.

"My secretary died half an hour ago," Dorey said, in a hard, tight voice. "She fell from her apartment window. The post mortem is being rushed through. There is a puncture mark on her arm. I think she has been injected with scopolamine. If she has, she has talked. Be very much on guard, Girland. I'm sending down six more men. On no account is Erica Olsen to be allowed out into the open. Do you understand? Don't let her out onto the terrace. It is just possible someone could snipe her from the Corniche if he was a first-class shot. She is to remain in the villa. This you must see to and I hold you responsible."

"Okay," Girland said. "I've already thought about the terrace. Is this Malik?"

"It must be, but I have no proof," Dorey said bitterly. "The roads and airport are being watched. If he heads south, I will let you know."

"I'll talk to O'Leary right away. I'll get him to put a man up on the Corniche."

"Do that."

"Oh, another thing. I want to see the file you have on Kung. Can you let me have it?"

"Why?"

"I know nothing about him. If she says something connected with him. I want as much information about him, to make sure she isn't talking nonsense, as I can get."

"Has she said anything yet?"

"She said something about a black grape."

"A grape?"

"Yes. I don't know what it means … it could mean nothing, but if she's going to let drop things like that, I want to be sure I'm not missing anything."

"Well, all right, I'll send the file down with O'Halloran's men. What exactly did she say about this grape?"

Girland told him.

"Hmm. Well, I don't know. Extraordinary. All right, Girland, keep at it and report to me anything else she comes out with," and Dorey hung up.

Girland left the villa and went down to the lodge. He told O'Leary what had happened.

"Get a man and a dog up on the Corniche. From up there, a class shot could pick us off like rabbits."

"Oh, no," O'Leary said firmly. "You're wrong. I've checked from the Corniche. There's no way down and the villa is completely screened from the road. If I had thought there was any danger from up there, I would have had a man there right away, but our rear is safe. Trouble is my business, Girland. You look after the woman. I'll take care of the trouble."

"I want a man and a dog up there," Girland said quietly. "It's an order, O'Leary."

The two men stared at each other, then O'Leary, his eyes sparkling with anger, said, "If that's what you want, then that's what you'll get." He paused, then added, "but it's a waste of a man."

"You're getting another six by tomorrow ... and that's what I want."

Girland returned to the villa and walked slowly up the stairs, his mind occupied. He paused at Erica Olsen's door, opened it quietly and looked into the room. She was sleeping, her blonde hair spread out on the pillow, her face with its classical beauty, relaxed and peaceful.

Girland closed the door and went along to the bathroom. He took a cold shower, then carrying his clothes, he walked the few paces to his bedroom and opened the door.

A small voice said, "Mark ... please ... don't put on the light."

He stood in the doorway, his clothes held against him, covering his nakedness.

"Ginny?"

"I don't care! I know I will lose you tomorrow. Once that woman is up, you will never even look at me." The moonlight coming through the slats in the wooden shutters gave him enough light to see Ginny sitting up in his bed, holding the sheet against her. "Please don't hate me."

"Ginny, darling, I could never hate you."

Girland moved across the room, dropped his clothes and sat on the bed. He pulled the sheet from her.

"But, Ginny, are you sure?" His arms went around her slim, naked body.

"I know I am shameless," she whispered, her fingers caressing his back, "because I am so very sure."

She was an irresistible gift that Girland took gently and with pleasure.

Malik and Smernoff completely fooled the police who were watching for them on all roads leading south. They drove rapidly to Le Touquet Airport, then chartered an air taxi to Aix-en-Provence Aero Club. There one of Smernoff's men was waiting for them in a fast car. They drove through Draguignan, Grasse, Tourettes and down to Cagnes-sur-Mer. Here, in a shabby villa by the sea which one of the Soviet Embassy's contacts owned, they sat around a table and Malik questioned Petrovka who Smernoff had alerted as soon as they suspected that Nice was the likely hiding place.

Petrovka, thin and young, with a burning ambition to be as successful as Malik, had gone to Dorey's villa while Malik and Smernoff were on their way down to Cagnes. His report was brief and to the point.

"The villa is impregnable," he said. "There is no way of breaking in except by a frontal attack. There are six heavily armed men guarding the place."

He then produced a sketch map of the villa which Malik studied. Malik lit a cigarette and pushed back his chair.

"This needs thinking about. A frontal attack is out of the question." He pointed to the map. "Are you sure we can't get down the mountain from the upper road? Is there no path?"

"There is no path shown on the local maps."

Malik made an impatient movement.

"That doesn't mean there isn't one. Go there at once and make sure."

Petrovka got to his feet.

"At once," he said and left.

Malik looked at Smernoff, his green eyes glittering.

"He should have checked. He is a fool."

Smernoff shrugged.

"Show me anyone as young as he who isn't a fool," he said. "I have to make do with what I can get."

There were a number of French and American tourists on the 7.30 a.m. flight from Paris to Nice which arrived at 8.55 a.m. Among them was a young Chinese girl who carried a violin case. She wore a cheap flowered dress and stiletto heel shoes. She walked a little awkwardly. She passed through the police barrier with the other tourists and then walked out into the lobby.

Jo-Jo, in a bad mood because he had had to get up so early, came over and joined her. He had no interest in Chinese women. He thought their short, thick legs unsightly and their hips so much lumps of meat.

"Have you got it?" he asked the girl as she paused before him.

"Yes."

"Then come on."

He walked out of the airport to where he had parked the 404. The girl followed him, stumbling a little, but very proud of her stiletto heels. They got in the car and Jo-Jo, driving carefully, headed for Villefranche.

Neither of them said anything during the drive to Ruby's hotel. Pearl greeted the girl. In the security of their bedroom, Sadu opened the violin case and took from it a .22 rifle, neatly in half, a telescopic sight and a silencer. The gun was a beautiful precision firearm made by a Japanese hand. He handed the gun to Jo-Jo.

"Well, there you are," he said. "I have done my job, now you do yours."

Jo-Jo carried the gun to the bed and sat down. He assembled the gun, screwed on the silencer, then clamped on the telescopic sight. Walking to the window, he aimed at a distant tree. His movements were so efficient and professional that Sadu felt a little chill in spite of the stuffiness of the room.

Jo-Jo turned and smiled. He seldom smiled, and his thin, vicious face became even more vicious as he showed his badly-discoloured teeth.

"It's a beaut," he said. "She is as good as dead."

6

A movement near him brought Girland abruptly awake.

"It's all right," Ginny said softly. "I'm going back to my room."

"What's the time?"

Just after six."

Girland sighed, stretched and turned on his back. Ginny, sitting on the edge of the bed, her blonde hair a little tousled, her naked back to him, was groping with her feet for her slippers.

He reached out and pulled her backwards across his chest.

"Hello, Ginny," he said. "Don't go yet." His hands closed over her small breasts and he kissed her ear.

She jerked away and scrambled clear of him. Snatching up her wrap, she put it on.

"No, please. I didn't mean to wake you."

Girland crossed his hands at the back of his neck and regarded her.

"It's early. Come here ... you don't have to rush away as if you're catching a train."

"No. It was a lovely night, Mark, but it is finished now. It won't happen again."

"It was a lovely night," Girland agreed, thinking how pretty she looked. Then with his charming smile, he said, "I would like it to happen again, Ginny, darling."

"No. You have a job to do, and so have I. This isn't the way to do it. Please don't make it difficult for me. I'm going to see Miss Olsen now," and she started for the door.

"Ginny ..."

She paused to look at him.

"You're quite right, of course, but this job won't last very long. Could we make a date for the future?"

"I thought you were twice my age, and I was much too young," Ginny said, regarding him seriously.

"I can put up with it if you can," Girland said, smiling.

"We'll see."

He cocked his eyebrow at her.

"Please don't make it difficult for me."

She tried to suppress a giggle, but failed.

"Well, the hospital won't run away, and that's where I work," she said and was gone.

Girland reached for a cigarette, lit it and relaxed back in the bed. He sighed contentedly. This, he decided, was the best job he had ever had from the CIA. So good it was suspicious. He blew a stream of smoke up to the ceiling and wondered how long it would be before Erica recovered her memory. He wondered too if she would give him the information Dorey wanted. He frowned, remembering those few strange words she had uttered: It is beautiful and black like a grape. Just what did that mean? Anything or nothing? Was this reference to a grape something to do with Kung's new weapon? He shook his head. It was unlikely: weapons weren't beautiful. Impatiently, he stubbed out his cigarette. He looked at the bedside clock. It was only 6.15 a.m. Too early yet to get up. He closed his eyes and let his mind recall the exciting moments of the night. You never knew with women, he thought. Who would have imagined there was so much passion locked up in that immature little body?

An hour later, still dozing, Girland heard a tap on the door and he called to come in.

Diallo entered with coffee and orange juice on a tray.

"What time would you like breakfast, sir?" he asked as he set down the tray.

Girland looked guiltily around the room to make sure Ginny had left no trace of her visit. He could see none.

"Another hour, I think," he said, stretching. "What have we got?"

"Eggs, sir, anyway you like them. The ham looks very good. If you fancy a blue trout, I can recommend it."

Girland sighed with ecstasy.

"I'll take the trout. Does Mr Dorey always live in this style?"

"What style, sir?" Diallo looked genuinely puzzled.

"That means he does," Girland said and shook his head in wonderment. "All right, Diallo. I'll be down in an hour."

An hour and thirty minutes later, breakfast finished, Girland was about to settle on the terrace with the *New York Herald Tribune* when Sergeant O'Leary came briskly up the steps. He had under his arm a fair sized parcel which was heavily sealed.

"This came for you," he said, putting the parcel on the table. "Will you sign for it?" As Girland signed the receipt, O'Leary went on, "Six more men have arrived. There's a man and a dog on the upper Corniche."

"Fine," Girland said. "Have some coffee?"

"I'm on duty," O'Leary said curtly and left the terrace.

Girland grimaced. He realised he had annoyed O'Leary by insisting on having a man on the Corniche. He shrugged.

Well, that was too bad. He couldn't afford to take chances, and besides, it had been an order from Dorey.

He got to his feet and opened the parcel which contained a bulky file on Feng Hoh Kung. He carried it into the living-room and locked it away in a drawer of the big desk standing on the alcove. Then he went up the stairs and knocked on Erica's bedroom door.

Ginny came to the door. She was wearing her nurse's uniform and she looked impersonally at him. She didn't even smile when he gave her a broad wink.

"How's the patient?" he asked, seeing she was determined to be impersonal.

"She's up and well," Ginny said. "She is asking to go out on the terrace. Please come in."

Girland moved past her into the big, pleasant room. Erica was sitting in a lounging chair by the open window that had a direct view of the sea. She was wearing a blue wrap which Girland guessed Ginny had bought for her, and as he came over to her, she turned her head and looked at him. She smiled and held out her hand.

"Hello, Mark," she said.

He kissed her fingers, aware that Ginny had left the room. Then he sat down in a chair nearby.

"How are you feeling this morning, Erica?"

"Wonderful. I want a swim. Will you take me?"

"Hey! Hey!" he said in mock alarm. "Not yet! Although I can't wait for you to get back to normal, you mustn't rush things. You must keep out of the sun."

She gazed at him and Girland thought how beautiful she looked.

"But I love the sun. It will do me good."

"You want to get your memory back, don't you? The doctor says on no account should you be in too strong a light. I know it is going to be a bore for you, but you must not even go out of doors for a few days. If you do, your memory will suffer." He wondered if she would accept this lie.

"I see." She grimaced. "Oh, well, I suppose ..." She again looked at him. "This is the strangest thing. I can't believe you are my husband. You really are my husband?"

"I can show you our marriage certificate if you want to be convinced," Girland said lightly and laughed. "Yes, darling, I really am your husband."

"And yet I remember nothing about you." She put her fingers lightly on the back of his hand. "You seem very nice ... just the kind of husband I would choose. How long have we been married?"

"Three years," Girland said glibly.

"Have we any children?"

"No."

"Why is that, Mark?"

He scratched the back of his neck, suddenly uneasy.

"We've been moving around ... we haven't had much chance to settle down."

"What is your business?"

"I work for IBM ... the computer people. Right now I am doing a deal here and I hired this villa while I'm fixing things."

"Where is here?" She seemed to be listening in an abstract kind of a way, but Girland had a feeling she was growing tense.

"Eze ... near Nice in France," he told her.

"Are you a very important person, Mark?"

"I wouldn't say that. I'm pretty successful. No more than that."

"Then why are there soldiers patrolling the garden with guns?"

Girland's brain worked quickly.

"I have a deal set up with the French Government," he said smoothly. "The Minister of Finance is coming here in a day or so. Someone threw a bomb at him last month. He is a little nervous. We called out the Army to give him confidence. It's all rather silly, but the deal is important. You don't have to worry about them."

He was watching her carefully. She seemed to relax a little.

"I see." She turned to look at him. The dark, violet-blue eyes searched his face. "I am glad you are my husband, Mark. You don't know what it means to lose the past the way I have lost it and then to find myself in this lovely room with someone like you."

Girland shifted.

"I understand. You'll recover your memory soon. You see ..."

"Did we ever quarrel?"

"Why, no. What should we quarrel about?"

"Married people do, don't they?"

He decided to shift the conversation which was becoming embarrassing to him to safe ground.

"Don't you remember one little thing of your past, Erica?" he asked. "Don't you even remember the trip we did a couple of months ago to Peking?"

She stiffened and her hands turned into fists.

"Peking?"

"Yes."

She sat for a long moment, staring out of the window.

"I didn't like Peking," she said in a cold, flat voice.

"Why do you say that?"

She made a movement of distaste.

"I don't know. It's something I feel. What happened to me in Peking?"

"Why, nothing. I was there on business," Girland lied. "You did a lot of sightseeing while I was busy. Don't you remember?"

"I don't want to talk about it. It is something unpleasant to me."

"But I thought you enjoyed it. Don't you remember those grapes?" Girland leaned forward. "The black ones ..."

She turned swiftly, her eyes suddenly bright and animated.

"There was one ... a beautiful thing. There was a golden dragon ... there was ..." Then her eyes went dull again and putting her hands to her head, she exclaimed, "Oh, why can't I remember! The grape is so important!"

"Why is it important?"

"I don't know, but I feel it is important. I had it with me ... I ..." She broke off, looking distressed.

"Well, don't worry about it," Girland said soothingly.

"Give it time." He got to his feet. "I'll see you again in a little while. I have a lot of work to do right now. Just relax and don't worry. Do you want something to read?"

"No. I want to think. I feel the more I think, the quicker I will remember."

"All right, but don't overtax yourself. I'll tell Nurse Roche to come up. She'll keep you company."

"Not now ... later, perhaps." She smiled at him and held out her hand. When he took it, she pulled him closer and offered him her lips. They kissed, then she leaned back. "All right, Mark, go and do your work. Come and see me again soon."

A trifle shaken, Girland left the room and walked down the stairs to the living-room. Ginny was glancing through the newspaper. She looked up at him inquiringly.

"Ginny, dear, there is one thing bothering me and we'll have to attend to it," Girland said. "Erica must have some clothes. Will you go to Nice right away and buy her whatever she should have? Better take Diallo with you. He has the money. Will you do that?"

"Of course," Ginny said.

When she had gone up to change, Girland went over to the desk, took out Kung's file and carrying it out onto the terrace, settled down to examine it.

Around midday, the traffic up to the Grande Corniche began to thicken. A stream of rubberneck buses, packed with tourists came crawling up the steep hill and along the curving road, stopping every now and then to allow photographic enthusiasts to snap their cameras out of the open windows.

Pfc Dave Fairfax sat in his Jeep which was parked in a lay-by and watched the traffic with a jaundiced eye. His receiving set played soft, swing music. The Alsatian police dog slept at the back of the Jeep.

Fairfax was not only bored, but irritated. Hadn't his Sergeant told him that sitting up on this goddam road was so much waste of time? How much more pleasant it would have been to be in the garden of the Villa where the other boys were. Some of them had organised a crap game, and Fairfax fancied himself as an expert. If he had been down there instead of up on this sun blistered road, he could have cleaned up, and he needed the money. There was that French chick he had run into on Villefranche harbour the other night. She was aching for it, but he knew instinctively what she would cost. The trouble was he had competition with the goddam Navy. Those guys certainly had it good. Once they got off that lump of iron anchored in the harbour, the chicks were all over them.

Three rubberneck buses moved slowly past him. An owl-faced man with thick horn-rimmed spectacles leaned out of the window and took a photograph of the Jeep. Fairfax made a face at him. He lifted one finger and stabbed the air with it. The owl-faced man grinned, and the bus moved on.

Fairfax shifted in his seat. It was hot. He thought longingly of the shady garden. It did him some good to watch the number of cars crawling behind the buses. The expressions of exasperation on the drivers' faces as they realised it wasn't possible to get by the line of buses amused Fairfax. At least he wasn't the only one to be suffering.

Convinced he was wasting his time, assured by O'Leary that there was no way for anyone to get down to the Villa from the Corniche, Fairfax was far from being alert. Every now and then, he dozed. After all, he argued, if the dog could sleep, why shouldn't he?"

He failed to notice, among the crawling traffic, a black 404. Had he been alert, he might have become curious at the sight of a pretty Vietnamese girl at the wheel. By her side was a slimly built man who looked half-Chinese. In the rear of the car was a young beatnik who lolled against the back of the seat, his small black eyes restless and glittering.

"On your left," Pearl said softly.

Sadu had already seen the Jeep. He stiffened and put his hand up to his face. Jo-Jo also looked at the Jeep. He saw an American soldier, his feet up on the dashboard, his jaw moving rhythmically as he chewed gum, his eyes half closed.

"Do you think they have found the path?" Sadu asked as Pearl brought the car to a stop in the traffic block.

"They may have. You'll have to go with him, Sadu," Pearl returned.

Sadu grimaced.

"You have my gun," Jo-Jo said. "I'll bring the rifle." Leaning forward, he dropped the silenced .38 into Sadu's lap.

Sadu hurriedly shoved the gun down the waistband of his trousers. He hated all this, but it was something he couldn't shirk.

"I'll stop at the next bend," Pearl said. "You will have to walk back. Don't forget the camera."

The traffic moved a little faster. Around the bend and out of sight of the soldier, Pearl began to slow down.

"Be quick," she said. "I'll be back in half an hour."

Sweating in the heat, Sadu grabbed the 16 mm movie camera he had brought with him, then slid back the catch on the door. Pearl put out her hand and signalled that she was stopping, then braked to a standstill. The long line of traffic behind her came to a slow, cursing halt.

Sadu and Jo-Jo slid out of the car and reached the narrow sidewalk as the driver behind the 404 blasted his horn. Pearl sent the car forward again.

The gun pressed painfully against his stomach as Sadu began to walk back. Jo-Jo, carrying the violin case and a rucksack containing food and wine, walked with him.

The path, overgrown and hidden from the road, was some hundred metres from the parked Jeep.

Sadu and Jo-Jo walked slowly towards the gap in the wall which led down to the path. They both felt like flies on a wall. There were no other pedestrians, and they were also aware that people in the crawling cars were looking at them. Sadu felt certain the violin case was attracting attention.

Jo-Jo said under his breath, "He's spotted us. Take some pictures."

Fairfax had just deposited his wad of gum on the undershelf of the Jeep's dashboard. He saw the two men, and for a brief moment, his mind became alert, then when one of them lifted a movie camera and began to take distant shots of the village below, he sneered to himself and began to peel the wrapping off another piece of gum.

Tourist! he thought. All the goddam equipment money can buy and I bet he takes lousy pictures!

A rubberneck bus was approaching.

"We go down the path when the bus is between him and us," Sadu said.

They waited. Sadu still pretended to take photographs.

Jo-Jo said, "Now ..."

Under the eyes of thirty tourists, but out of view of the Jeep, they quickly slid down the steep slope, through the undergrowth, moving dangerously quickly until they reached the path itself.

Sadu pulled the gun from his waistband and began to move forward. Jo-Jo waited for a few seconds before he followed him. When they were in sight of the villa's roof and when Sadu had satisfied himself there was no guard to worry them, he stopped.

"It's all right," he said. "They haven't found it. I'll get back. You must find your own way back to the hotel. Stay here until the job's done."

Jo-Jo grunted, moved past Sadu and continued on down the path. Sadu turned and began the climb back to the road.

He was lucky. A long line of rubberneck buses were passing and Fairfax, trying to get a change of programme on the receiving set had completely forgotten the two men taking photographs.

Jo-Jo now reached a spot where he could look down at the Villa's terrace which was deserted. He dropped his haversack and squatting on his heels, he rested his back against a tree. He felt concealed and safe. He spent the next few minutes assembling the rifle. He took aim at the terrace. The telescopic sight was so powerful he could easily make out the cracks in the paving stones. Satisfied, he loaded the gun, then with the gun across his knees, he settled down to wait.

While he waited, Henri Dumaine who ran a successful Insurance and Estate Agency business in Eze village was regarding Petrovka without much interest. He did not think this young, shabbily dressed man could have enough money to buy land in his district, but at the same time, he told himself, he might be acting as an agent for someone with money so he decided to be helpful.

"Yes, of course, I know Monsieur Dorey's villa," he said. "There are no villas in this district I do not know. You are interested in buying land above the villa?"

"Yes," Petrovka said. He had already been out to the Grande Corniche and he had seen the Jeep and the soldier. He had decided it was unsafe to search for a path with the soldier on guard, and in desperation, he had gone to the Estate Agent.

"Well, it is not impossible, of course. There is land for sale there, but I should tell you there is no water."

"That could be arranged," Petrovka said in his careful French. "I would like to look at the land. Is there a path down to the Villa?"

"There was a path," Dumaine told him. "At least, I think so." He got up and crossed to his filing cabinet. He took from it a number of sketch maps. "Yes, indeed, but I don't advise you to make use of it. It is dangerous. No one ever uses it now, and the soil must be loose."

"Could I see the map?" Petrovka asked, sweat breaking out under his arms. So he had failed! he was thinking. There was a path and he had told Malik there was no path.

Shrugging, Dumaine handed the map across the desk.

Petrovka studied it. He saw at a glance that he had passed the opening to the path which was close to where the Jeep had been parked.

He made a mental note of the opening down to the path, then returned the map.

"It might be interesting," he said and got to his feet. "I will let you know."

Dumaine was scarcely able to disguise his disgust.

"As you will, monsieur," he said, rose, bowed, shook hands and watched Petrovka depart.

Petrovka drove back to the Grande Corniche. He was uneasy and unhappy. He knew he had wasted valuable time. Glancing at his cheap watch, he saw it was now 1.10 p.m. Malik would be waiting impatiently for his report. But since the path did exist, he must get details.

The traffic had slackened and he drove past the Jeep without difficulty. A few metres further on, there was a lay-by. He pulled into it and turned off the car's engine.

There was now this problem of exploring the path without the sentry seeing him. He got out of the car and walked briskly back along the narrow sidewalk until he reached the bend in the road. Then waiting until there was a lull in the traffic, he climbed over the wall and lowered himself down onto the mountain side. He had a dangerous and difficult scramble to where the path was, but he managed it. Every now and then, his feet slipped, and he thought he was going to fall, but by grabbing a shrub here and thudding against a tree trunk there, he finally managed to reach the path without being seen.

He began a cautious descent.

Relaxing in the sun, Jo-Jo heard him coming. His first warning was a stone that came rattling past him. He got silently to his feet, snatched up the haversack and moved off the path into the thick undergrowth. He waited, crouching, his lips drawn off his discoloured teeth, his finger around the trigger of his gun.

Then he saw Petrovka, a Mauser 7.63 mm gun in his hand, coming cautiously down the path. Jo-Jo lifted the rifle. It was an easy shot. The .22 bullet smashed into Petrovka's forehead and he died without a sound.

Jo-Jo wiped the sweat from his face, reloaded the rifle, then walking to Petrovka's dead body, he dragged it into the scrub.

In the drab little villa at Cagnes, Malik waited, pacing up and down. Smernoff, sitting at the open window, watched the girls in their bikinis, displaying themselves on the beach.

It wasn't until Girland was nearly at the end of Feng Hoh Kung's file that he suddenly became alert. He began to read a cutting from *The Art & The Connoisseur*, dated 1937 that was clipped into the file.

Up to this moment he had ploughed through a mass of uninteresting reports from various Agents, a summary of Kung's character, his past achievements, his general background and his present work. Then suddenly this article from a defunct magazine caught his interest.

The article stated that over the centuries the Kung family had been collectors of rare antiques, precious stones and jade and Feng Hoh Kung had inherited all these treasures.

"Among this amazing collection, second to none in the world," the article went on, "is the famous Black Grape, the only known jet black pearl in existence. The pearl originally belonged to Shi Huang-ti who built the Great Wall of China in the 3rd Century, BC. It was acquired by the Kung family in 1753 and has remained with the family ever since."

Girland pushed the file aside, reached for a cigarette and stared out onto the sunlit terrace.

This, he thought, was what Erica had been talking about. *It is beautiful and black like a grape.* She had probably seen the pearl and it had made a big impression. He shrugged and again pulled the file towards him. Then he paused, his dark eyes narrowing. He remembered her sudden agitation and what she had said: *I had it with me.*

Was there a possible chance that she really had the pearl? Was this the reason why she had left Kung? He re-read the article and then sitting back, he rubbed the side of his jaw while he thought.

He had many contacts. He was now asking himself who could tell him more about the Black Grape. His mind raced over the names of his contacts, then he snapped his fingers. He remembered Jacques Yew who owned a successful Oriental shop on the Boulevard des Moulins, Monte Carlo. Some years ago, Yew had run into trouble with one of his many boys who had turned vicious and had been trying to blackmail him. Girland had met Yew by chance in a Paris cellar club. Bored with waiting for a girl who hadn't turned up, Girland had listened to Yew's tale of woe. Blackmail was something that disgusted Girland. He handled the boy who was threatening Yew, reducing him to a terrified wreck, and Yew had said if Girland ever wanted his help, he could call on him.

This was the way Girland lived. He performed a service and never hesitated to collect payment later. Now, he thought, Yew could be useful.

He locked the file away. The time was 12.30 p.m. He would see Yew that afternoon. Ginny should be back at any moment. Erica had been on her own for more than two hours. A little reluctantly, Girland went upstairs, tapped on her door and entered.

Erica, still sitting by the window, turned and smiled at him.

"Have you finished work, Mark?" she asked, holding out her hand to him.

"For the moment." He came over and kissed her fingers. "But I have to go out this afternoon. Have you been bored?"

"No, I have been thinking." There was a pause, then she asked, "Mark ... have we been in Paris lately?"

"Yes. We have just come from Paris. Why do you ask?"

"My mind is walking through clouds. Sometimes the clouds get thinner and then I can see where I am walking. Do you understand?"

"Of course. Do you remember Paris?"

"I remember I stayed at a hotel. You weren't with me."

"What was the hotel?"

She didn't hesitate as she said, "Hotel Astorg."

"Your clothes are missing. They could be at the hotel. I had better telephone them."

She frowned.

"What happened in Paris?"

"I don't know. We were staying at George V. I went out on business. When I returned you had gone with your luggage."

"Do you think I was planning to run away from you?"

Girland smiled.

"I don't think so. You probably woke up after I had gone, found you had lost your memory, got frightened and walked out."

She shook her head helplessly.

"I suppose so. Would you telephone the hotel? I would like to have my things."

"I'll do it now. Nurse Roche is in Nice at the moment getting you something to wear. I'll be right back."

Downstairs, he put a call through to Dorey. When Dorey came on the line, Girland said, "She stayed at the Astorg Hotel. She could have left her luggage there."

"So she's beginning to talk?"

"Looks like it."

"Has she come out with anything else?"

Girland thought of the Black Grape. He hesitated, then said, "Not so far."

"I'll get O'Halloran to check the hotel. All right at your end?"

Thinking of the service he was getting, Girland said, "I'm not complaining."

"I don't want complications with you and this woman or with the nurse. Do you understand?"

"I get the drift," Girland said and grinned. "Any news of Malik?"

"No, but he hasn't gone south."

"Where is he then?"

"I don't know. For the moment we have lost track of him, but I am satisfied he hasn't gone south."

"You and who else?" Girland asked mockingly. "If you have lost track of him, then it's a safe bet he is right here," and he hung up.

He went out onto the terrace, watched by Jo-Jo in his hide-out on the mountain side, walked down the steps and talked to Sergeant O'Leary. He warned O'Leary that Malik might be preparing for an attack. O'Leary said everything was under control and that trouble was his business. Girland regarded him thoughtfully, resisted a sarcastic retort and as he began to return to the villa, Ginny with Diallo came driving through the gateway.

Ginny was wearing a big sun hat that hid her face and her hair and Jo-Jo, staring through the telescopic sight wondered if she was Erica Olsen or some visitor. He mustn't make a mistake, he told himself. He had been told that Erica was tall and blonde. He had plenty of time. He would only have one shot.

While Diallo was preparing a quick lunch, Girland and Ginny went up to Erica's room.

"Here's Nurse Roche," Girland said. "She has some clothes for you. I called the hotel. They will be calling back."

"Thank you, Mark." Erica got to her feet. Girland's expression of admiration as he looked at her was not lost on Ginny who began to unpack the suitcase she had with her.

An hour later, Girland drove into Monte Carlo. Parking the car with some difficulty, he walked briskly along Boulevard des Moulins and entered Jacques Yew's shop.

Yew was sitting at an ornate desk examining a piece of jade he was planning to sell to a rich American tourist staying at the Hotel de Paris. He was a small, thin, effeminate looking man with sandy hair and artistic features. He stared for a moment as Girland came to rest at his desk, then recognising him, he jumped to his feet, his face lighting up with a genuine smile of welcome.

"My dear boy! How good it is to see you again!" He offered a small limp hand. "Sit down. What are you doing in this ghastly little village?"

"On vacation. How are you, Jacques?"

Yew grimaced, then shrugged.

"So-so. Business is bad and that always depresses me. There is no real money about these days. And how are you?"

"I'm fine." Girland paused to light a cigarette, then went on, "Can I ask you a question without you asking me one?"

Yew looked bewildered.

"What an odd request. Yes, of course. What is the question?"

"Have you ever heard of the Black Grape pearl?"

Yew's small eyes opened wide.

"Well, of course. It belongs to the Kung family and at the moment it is in Peking. What ...?"

"Remember? No questions, Jacques. Tell me about it."

"Well, it is, of course, utterly unique. It belonged to Shi Huang-ti who you may know built the Great Wall. It was supposed to have been found by a fisherman in an oyster bed off the Persian Gulf. This was around the 3rd Century BC. It isn't known how it got into the Kung family's hands. Around 1887 the present Kung's father compiled an illustrated catalogue of his treasures and this was the first time dealers and collectors knew the Black Grape was in the Kung's collection." He got to his feet and walked over to a bookcase crammed with Art books. "I have a copy of the catalogue somewhere." He searched for a moment, then pulled out a heavy volume bound in white vellum and brought it to the desk. He flicked through the pages, then turned the book to face Girland. "Here's a photograph of the pearl. It is absolutely unique."

Girland studied the photograph. It showed a jet black pearl, the size of a large grape, resting on the back of a Chinese dragon carved in gold.

"I had no idea a real black pearl existed," Girland said, studying the photograph.

"There are lots of so-called black pearls, although in fact they are grey. This is the only real black pearl. There is a theory for what it is worth that the oyster became impregnated by the ink from an octopus. Just a theory, but an interesting one. The dragon is also a beautiful piece." Yew put the book away, then turned and regarded Girland. "I must say, my dear boy, your interest in this pearl raises my curiosity."

"What's it worth?" Girland asked, tapping ash into the silver ashtray on Yew's desk.

"Worth?" Yew smiled wistfully. "You couldn't put a price to it. If it came up for auction, the collectors of the world would scramble for it. I doubt if enough money exists these days to buy it."

"But suppose Kung wanted to sell?" Girland asked. "Suppose he was short of cash. What could you sell it for?"

Yew shook his head.

"I wouldn't attempt to sell it. It is much too important a piece. It should go to Christies for the world to bid for it."

"But suppose this had to be an undercover deal? Suppose Kung didn't want his government to know about the sale. Do you know a collector who would buy it?"

Yew regarded Girland thoughtfully, his eyes suddenly hooded.

"Yes, I know three or four collectors who would buy it."

"What kind of price?"

Yew shrugged.

"That's not easy. I would try for three million dollars."

Girland drew in a long, slow breath.

"Think you would get it?"

"It is possible."

"The whole affair would be arranged without publicity?"

"That is also possible."

"It would have to be."

Again Yew regarded Girland.

"My friend," he said, "I can't believe you are wasting your time talking this way unless you know more than you are telling me. Why not be frank? You can trust me. I am your friend. Are you acting for Kung? Does he really want to sell his pearl?"

Girland got to his feet.

"Don't let's rush this, Jacques," he said. "Thanks for the information. If you had the pearl, you could sell it for three million dollars ... right?"

Yew touched his temple with a silk handkerchief.

"Yes."

"Fine ... I'll be seeing you." Girland shook hands and walked out of the shop.

He was in a very thoughtful mood as he drove back to Eze.

... In the shabby villa at Cagnes, Malik paced up and down.

"What is happening to the fool?" he demanded, his voice vicious with rage. "He has been gone three hours! What is he doing?"

Smernoff sighed and dragged his eyes away from a suntanned girl in a white bikini who was running down to the sea.

"The traffic is bad," he said. "It would take an hour to get up the Corniche and an hour to get back. Don't be so impatient." He pointed. "That girl ... look at the length of her legs. She is really very pleasing. I would like to ..."

"Shut up!" Malik barked. "Go and look for him, Boris. Go up to the Corniche and find out what he is doing!"

Smernoff recognised the dangerous note in Malik's voice. He got to his feet and moved to the door.

"It will take me some time, but I will go," he said.

Impatiently, Malik waved him away. When Smernoff had gone, Malik sat in the chair Smernoff had been using. He looked out onto the beach. The girl in the white bikini was walking along the beach, swinging her bathing cap.

Malik watched her.

O'Halloran came into Dorey's office. He carried a blue and white suitcase which he put on a chair.

"This is hers," he said as Dorey put aside a file and got to his feet. "The hotel had it in their left luggage office. She told them she would collect it later."

"I thought you said there were two suitcases?" Dorey said.

"There were. I haven't traced the other yet. There's nothing of interest in this one. Just clothes. I've been through it. Good, expensive stuff, but nothing to help us."

Dorey showed his disappointment. He shrugged and sat down.

"How about the second suitcase?"

"Could be anywhere. We are working with Dulay and he is having every left luggage locker checked and is checking all left luggage offices. It's a big job. Could take days."

"How did she register at the hotel?"

"As Naomi Hill from Los Angeles. There is no doubt she is the woman. I showed the staff at the hotel her photograph. They immediately recognised her."

"How about her passport?"

"The reception clerk didn't see it. She told him her passport was in her luggage. She took the police card and filled it in herself. I'm checking the passport number. It's certain to be a false one."

"Doesn't look as if she had lost her memory at that time, does it?" Dorey said thoughtfully. "Looks as if she was on the run."

"I suppose we are sure she really has lost her memory?" O'Halloran said.

"Dr Forrester seems certain about it. She might be faking." Dorey sat for a moment in thought. "I'll talk to Girland. In the meantime if you are sure there is nothing in the suitcase of value, you had better put it on a plane and let her have it."

"There's nothing."

"Well, then do that." Dorey reached for the telephone. Ten minutes later, he was talking to Girland. He told him one of the suitcases had been found.

"There's nothing of interest in it for us," Dorey went on. "I'm having it sent down to the Nice Airport. You can get someone to collect it. O'Halloran and I have been talking about this woman." He went on to tell Girland that she had registered under the name of Naomi Hill of Los Angeles. "We are wondering if she really has lost her memory or is faking. I want you to lay a trap for her."

"Such as how?" Girland asked, reaching for a cigarette.

"Call her Naomi. Watch her closely. See if you get any reaction," Dorey said. "Do you want me to send someone down there to handle it?"

Girland, thinking about the Black Grape, said, "No. I can handle it. Give me an hour or so. I'll think what is best to do. I have an idea she isn't faking, but you might be right," and he hung up.

Ginny, who had been listening to all this, said, "She isn't faking, Mark. I am quite sure of it. I've had a loss of memory case before now. There is this lost, vague look in the eyes that can't be faked."

Girland smiled at her.

"I don't think she is faking. My boss was born suspicious. I'm going up to talk to her. Why don't you go out on the terrace and top up your beautiful sun tan?"

Ginny looked at him, then nodded.

"All right." She paused, then went on, "She is lovely, isn't she?"

He crossed the room and put his arms around her.

"So are you, Ginny. You have something she hasn't."

Ginny touched his cheek with her finger.

"What is that?"

"I'll tell you tonight."

She moved away from him. Girland watched her. She wandered to the French windows leading out onto the terrace, paused, then looked at him.

"All right ... then tell me tonight," she said and walked out into the hot sunshine.

Jo-Jo was feeling the heat. He had already drunk half the bottle of wine Ruby had given him, and he now decided it had been a mistake to drink wine. It only made him hotter. He should have brought Coca-Cola. He had taken off his dirty, cotton coat and had rolled up his black shirt sleeves. Sweat sparkled on his narrow forehead as he shifted further into the shade. He had been up on the mountain now for four hours and the terrace had been deserted for all this time. He pulled the haversack towards him, looked into it and took out a demi-baguette, split in two and filled with ham and garlic sausage. He gnawed a piece off, wiped the sweat from his face and began chewing. The rifle across his knees felt hot. Suddenly he stiffened. He spat out the half-eaten lump of bread and lifted the rifle.

Here she was, and at last! he thought as far below him a blonde girl came out onto the terrace. She had on a skimpy sun suit and she sat on one of the lounging chairs. She began to spray her arms with a suntan bomb.

Jo-Jo, his mouth now dry, his body tense, lifted the rifle and peered at the girl through the telescopic sight. He had been told the woman was blonde. He knew the nurse was brunette. So this must be Erica Olsen. His lips came off his discoloured teeth and he held his breath as the cross section of the sight centred on the girl's' forehead. She had paused and was looking down into the garden, motionless. Jo-Jo knew he was being offered the perfect target. Very gently, still holding his breath, he squeezed the trigger.

7

Had Pfc Willy Jackson not been a light heavyweight champion, his life could easily have been made unbearable by the kidding and leg-pulling of his companions. But since Jackson could lick any man in his battalion, and since he was in an ugly and sullen mood, no one attempted to kid him about the way he had let the Commies walk off with this Swedish chick.

Jackson had recovered consciousness with a bruised and swollen jaw in the Bois. He had been reprimanded and was now on sentry detail at Dorey's villa, the bruise on his jaw turning a pale yellow and green.

Sergeant O'Leary sent him up onto the Corniche to relieve Pfc Fairfax. The change of guard took place at 1 p.m., and now Jackson with his police dog, was taking his duties seriously.

He had been given a black mark by his Commanding Officer and that had hurt Jackson's feelings. He decided that anyone acting suspiciously on this sun-roasted road should be challenged. He didn't even sit in the Jeep nor did he allow his dog to sleep. Jackson was breathing fire and was very much on the ball.

A little after 1.30 p.m. with the traffic crawling past him in a steady stream, Jackson saw a young beatnik, carrying a violin case on the narrow sidewalk which ran along the low wall of the mountain side.

A few moments previously, there had been a gap in the traffic, and Jackson had had a clear view of the long strip of the Corniche he was guarding. There had been no pedestrians in sight, and now this young beatnik had materialised from nowhere.

Jackson hesitated only for a moment, then he shouted, "Hey, you! Just a moment!"

Jo-Jo flinched, but kept walking. He controlled the urge to run and looked as casually as he could at the distant view as if he hadn't heard Jackson's shout.

"You!"

Jo-Jo kept on.

Jackson snapped his fingers at his dog and pointed. The dog was out of the Jeep like a black flash, whipped in front of a crawling car, got ahead of Jo-Jo and planted itself in front of him. Jo-Jo came to an abrupt halt. There was something deadly in the way the dog stared up at him. For the first time in his short vicious life, Jo-Jo knew fear.

Carrying his automatic rifle at the alert, Jackson crossed the road, his eyes coldly suspicious. He came up to Jo-Jo.

"Didn't you hear me tell you to stop?" he demanded in his excruciating French.

"Why should I stop for you, Yank?" Jo-Jo said, licking his dry lips.

"What have you got in there?" Jackson said, pointing his rifle at the violin case.

"A violin, and what's it to you? Listen, Yank, I don't know what you think you're doing. I'm a French subject. Take your dog and get lost."

"Where did you come from?"

"What's it to you?"

"You've come up the mountain side, haven't you?"

"What should I be doing on the mountain side?" Jo-Jo

sneered. "If you don't want to land yourself in trouble, you'd better leave me alone. I'm a French subject and ..."

"I heard you the first time. Open that fiddle case!"

If it hadn't been for the dog, Jo-Jo would have whipped out his knife, stabbed this fool and made a bolt for it. But the dog made this impossible. Jo-Jo was really scared of the dog.

"You don't talk this way to me, Yank," he said. "Get the hell out of my way."

Jackson hesitated. He realised he had no right to interfere with a French subject, but this dirty, vicious looking little rat had come up the mountainside. He was sure of that and he wasn't going to let him go.

"Look, sonny, why don't you act sensibly? If you have nothing to hide, open the fiddle case and you can go. It's as simple as that."

"I don't open anything for a goddamn Yank," Jo-Jo snarled.

Then out of the crawling traffic appeared a French road cop, immaculate in his white helmet, his blue uniform and his glittering knee-high boots.

Jackson waved to him.

Dropping his violin case, Jo-Jo, frantic now, made a grab at Jackson's automatic rifle. Two things happened to him at once. Jackson's left fist thudded against his jaw and the dog pounced, pinning his right wrist.

Girland tapped on Erica's door. She called for him to come in. He opened the door, then paused in the doorway.

Erica was dressed. She had on a black and green sleeveless frock and she was standing in front of a full-length mirror admiring herself. She turned and smiled at him.

"Well?"

Girland, who adored beautiful women, was for a brief moment so full of admiration that he said nothing, but just looked at her. Then he came into the room, closed the door and walked over to her.

"You look wonderful. That dress ... it suits you beautifully."

She again looked at herself in the mirror.

"I think it does." She came to him and put her long fingers on his arm. "Mark, can't I go out into the sun? I am sure I will feel so much better if only I could."

"Not yet. Please be patient. Come and sit down. I want to talk to you."

She sat down away from the window, crossed her long, shapely legs and looked inquiringly at him.

"Yes, Mark?"

"I want to try to help your memory," Girland said. He took a chair near hers. "Does the name Naomi Hill mean anything to you?"

She frowned, thought, then shook her head.

"No ... should it mean anything to me?"

From the despairing expression in her blue eyes, Girland was satisfied she wasn't faking.

"Never mind. The one thing you do seem to remember is this black grape."

Her eyes lit up.

"Yes. It keeps coming into my mind, but it isn't a grape, Mark. I think it's a pearl."

"That's right," Girland said. "It is a pearl, and it is set on the back of a Chinese dragon."

She stared at him, then nodded.

"Yes ... I remember that now. Do you know about it?"

"I know a little about it. Have you got it, Erica?"

She moved uneasily. "Should I have it?"

"I think so. Try to remember. It belonged to Feng Hoh Kung."

He could see from her expression the struggle going on in her mind. Finally, she threw up her hands.

"It's no use. It is like trying to open a door that won't open. There is a black pearl. I do know that. Kung ... does he live in Peking?"

"Yes."

"Let me think for a moment." She got up and walked slowly to the open window. Girland watched her. He saw her look down onto the terrace. He saw her stiffen, lean forward, stare, then her hands went to her face and she gave a loud piercing scream that set Girland's nerves tingling.

She spun around, horror in her eyes.

"What's the matter with her? Something's happened to her!"

Girland reached the window in two strides. He looked down onto the terrace where Ginny lay on the chaise-longue. He felt his heart kick against his side.

Ginny lay in an unnatural position. From where he stood, Girland could just make out a tiny red hole in the centre of her forehead. From it oozed a line of blood that ran down the side of her nose, across her parted lips and dripped onto her white sun suit.

As he turned and started for the door, Erica gave a low, gasping sigh and fell at his feet in a faint.

At the sound of the bell, Malik snatched up the telephone receiver. He had been sitting in the hot, stuffy little room of the villa now for three hours and he was in a white heat of fury.

"Boris," Smernoff said over the line. "Things have been

happening. The woman is dead. The police are looking for us. Do nothing until I get back," and he hung up.

Malik slowly replaced the receiver. He contained his fury with an effort that brought thick veins out on his forehead. He lit another cigarette and continued to wait.

Half an hour later, Smernoff came into the room.

"Well?"

"There was a path at the back of the villa," Smernoff said. "Petrovka found it. He walked into an ambush and he's dead. The police have picked up Jo-Jo Chandy, Yet Sen's agent. They caught him with a .22 rifle. He killed the woman with a long distance shot."

"Are you certain it was the woman?" Malik demanded, glaring at Smernoff.

"There was only one blonde woman in the villa. The nurse was dark. This blonde woman was on the terrace and Chandy picked her off like a sitting duck. Dorey's flying down ..."

Malik stared down at his powerful hands, his face wooden. "This is our first failure, Boris," he said. "We could be in trouble."

"There is always a first time," Smernoff said philosophically. He was glad this was Malik's responsibility. He couldn't see how he himself could be blamed. "What do we do now?"

"I must be absolutely certain this woman is dead," Malik said, "Get one of your men to talk to the Press."

"I have already arranged that. He should be calling any moment now."

Five minutes later, the call came through. Smernoff listened, grunted and then said, "You can return to Paris," and he hung up. Turning to Malik, he went on, "There's no doubt about it. The reporter for *Nice Matin* has seen the body. The dead woman is Erica Olsen."

Malik shrugged.

"Then we leave at once." He crossed the room and picking up the telephone receiver, he called Kovski at the Russian Embassy.

While he was breaking the news to Kovski, Dorey arrived at his villa. He came by military aircraft and by fast car from Nice. It was probably the fastest journey he had ever made in his life.

Girland, his eyes bleak and his face pale, explained what had happened. "O'Halloran's men didn't take the job seriously," he concluded bitterly. "Chandy and Malik's man got past the guards on the Corniche. That's something for you to sort out, but I want you to remember that this sentry is responsible for Ginny Roche's death."

"All right ... all right," Dorey said impatiently. He wasn't interested in Ginny Roche. "What about Erica Olsen?"

Girland ignored this.

"At least the French police are efficient. They have made Chandy talk, and they are picking up his two pals. They all work for Yet-Sen."

"Never mind that. That is a police affair. Is this woman talking yet?"

Girland looked at him in disgust.

"You have a one track mind, haven't you? It means nothing to you that that kid is dead. Well, she isn't talking. She's in shock. She saw Ginny murdered."

Dorey moved impatiently around the room. Girland watched him, then he said, "I have told the press the murdered woman is Erica Olsen."

Dorey paused and peered at Girland over the top of his glasses.

"Will they believe it?"

"They do believe it. The *Nice Matin* man is a friend of mine. I let him see the body. I told him she was the mysterious woman who had lost her memory. He didn't question it. When the Russians and the Chinese hear Erica Olsen is dead, they will lift the pressure. We can't go on the way we have been going on. I'm taking Erica out of here. She will leave as Nurse Roche. I'm getting her a dark wig and she'll wear Ginny's uniform. Once I get her away from here and the guards, I am sure I can get her to talk."

Dorey studied him suspiciously.

"Where are you taking her?"

"To an apartment in Monte Carlo. I have made all the necessary arrangements. She will be safe there for a week or so. Look, Dorey, it was your bright idea I should pretend to be her husband. She now accepts this fact, so you are stuck with your idea. You take care of the funeral, give it all the publicity you can and I'll take care of Erica. All I need is money. Give me a hundred thousand francs. She thinks I am a successful businessman and I have to act the part."

"Where is the apartment?"

Girland scribbled an address on a scratch pad, tore off the sheet and gave it to Dorey.

"Don't telephone me unless it is urgent. When she talks, I'll call you."

Dorey hesitated. He decided the idea might work and he couldn't think of an alternative. He would have been very uneasy had he overheard the telephone conversation between Girland and Jacques Yew that had taken place half an hour before he had arrived at the villa. In that conversation, Girland had asked Yew if he could accommodate a girl and himself in his apartment overlooking the Beach hotel. He also asked Yew to buy a woman's brown wig and to come with it at 5.30 p.m. to Dorey's villa.

Girland had concluded the conversation by saying, "You remember what I was saying, Jacques, about a grape? This has to do with it. Your co-operation now could put you right in the middle of a deal."

Jacques had said, "You can rely on me, dear boy. Of course you can use my apartment. You can have anything else you want."

But Dorey didn't know of this conversation; all the same he was a little dubious about Girland's plan.

"Nurse Roche could have relations," he said. "We can't bury her as Erica Olsen."

"I will only want a week. There'll be an inquest. Delay it as long as you can," Girland said impatiently. "If I can't get Erica talking in a week, then I never will."

"Isn't she remembering anything yet?"

"She remembered staying at the Astorg hotel. You have her suitcase."

"There were two suitcases. We have only found one."

Girland looked sharply at Dorey. "Two suitcases?"

"She left Peking with two. She had them with her at Hong Kong. O'Halloran is trying to trace the second one, but so far, without success."

Girland shrugged.

"I want some money. I'll need at least a hundred thousand francs."

"I will give you twenty thousand, and you will have to account for every franc," Dorey said firmly, and sitting down, he took out his chequebook.

"That's my Dorey," Girland said in disgust. "Mean in every emergency."

"Not mean … careful," Dorey said and signed the cheque with a flourish.

Sadu Mitchell sat in Ruby's little garden, his eyes going constantly to his wristwatch. It was now seven hours since he had left Jo-Jo on the mountain path. He was worried and uneasy. Pearl, relaxed, waited with oriental calm which irritated Sadu.

Suddenly they both heard Ruby's high-pitched voice crying out in alarm. They looked at each other. Sadu started to his feet, his fingers closing over the butt of Jo-Jo's gun.

"What is it?" Pearl said, without moving.

Ruby's cry of alarm abruptly ceased.

There was a moment of silence, more sinister than when she had been screaming. Sadu cursed, kicked away his chair and drew the gun.

"Drop it!" a man's voice snapped from the open French window.

In a panic, Sadu fired blindly in the direction of the voice.

Then he heard the bang of gunfire and felt a violent blow on his chest. He found himself lying on the hot, dry grass. He tried to lift his gun, but he had no strength left and the gun slipped from his grasp.

He looked wildly at Pearl who was sitting motionless, her pretty face expressionless, then he became aware of a pair of black, highly-polished jackboots just in range of his darkening vision.

By 5 p.m. the activity at the villa had died down. Dorey had gone with Inspector Dulay to the Nice Police Station. Ginny's body had been taken away in an ambulance. The newspaper men had gone. Sergeant O'Leary had taken his men in three Jeeps to the Airport.

Diallo, wide-eyed and nervous, Erica Olsen and Girland

were at last on their own.

From time to time, Girland had gone into Erica's room where she was lying on the bed, her back turned, her face hidden.

Girland didn't speak to her. He felt it best to wait for her to make her own recovery.

At 5.30 p.m. he saw Jacques Yew's black Cadillac come up the drive and he went out onto the terrace to greet him.

Carrying a paper bag, Yew climbed the steps and the two men went over to lounging chairs, shaded by a sun umbrella. They sat down.

"I don't know what this is all about, dear boy," Yew said, putting the bag on the table. "Here is the wig you asked me for. You are being intriguingly mysterious."

"It's intriguing all right," Girland said and went on to tell him the story of Erica Olsen.

"There is just a possible chance she may have the pearl," he concluded. "If she has, I think I could persuade her to cut us in. You handling the deal, and I getting a cut for putting her in touch with you."

Yew sat back, his hooded eyes glittering.

"What makes you think she has the pearl?" he asked.

"I'm playing a hunch. The one thing that gets her animated is the pearl. Now a pearl is easy to conceal. If I happened to be the mistress of an old Chinese goat and couldn't see much future in it, I would look around for something worthwhile to take before I walked out on him. That's how I would reason and I'm playing a hunch that is the way she has reasoned too."

"My dear boy! That's terribly dishonest!" Yew protested for a moment genuinely shocked.

"Yes," Girland grinned. "But if I'm right, and if she has

the pearl, will you sell it for her?"

"Of course I will," Yew said without hesitation.

"Fine. I'll bring her to your apartment in about an hour. I have my own car, so you needn't wait. Did you see any newspaper men on your way up?"

"There was no one."

"Okay, then you get off. We'll be joining you in about an hour."

"You really think she has the pearl? It seems unbelievable."

"I'm playing a hunch. Anyway, what can we lose?"

Yew looked dubious. "Well ... yes, I suppose that's right."

He gave Girland a Yale key. "That's the key of my apartment. You will have it to yourselves. I will stay with my brother. There is a woman who comes in every day. You can get your meals sent in. Is there anything else?"

"No, and thanks, Jacques. We could make some money out of this if we have any luck."

Girland thought for a moment, then repeated, "If we have any luck."

When Yew had driven away, Girland went up to Erica's room, taking the paper bag with him.

He tapped on the door and entered.

Erica was sitting now in a lounging chair. Her face was tense and white and she regarded him with a disconcerting stare.

"Well, darling?" he said as he closed the door. "How are you feeling?"

"You can cut that darling stuff out," she said in a flat, hard voice. "I don't know who you are, but I do know you are not my husband."

Girland smiled. "That's a relief," he said and came over

to sit opposite her.

"So you are getting your memory back?"

"I'm getting it back. What happened to her?"

"She thought she would look more attractive as a blonde," Girland said soberly. "They mistook her for you and they killed her."

Erica flinched. "And you? Who are you?"

"I guess I had better fill you in," Girland said.

He paused to light a cigarette, then went on. "You were found unconscious in Paris. You were taken to the American hospital. When they put you in bed, they found three tattoo marks on your body ... Chinese initials. Some bright boy reported this to the CIA. They put two and two together and decided you must be Erica Olsen, the mistress of Feng Hoh Kung, the top missile expert in Peking. The CIA wants all the information they can get about Kung. They dreamed up an idea. I was to be your husband and you were to tell me all about Kung. But the Chinese and the Russians heard about the tattoo marks and they also decided you must be Erica Olsen. The Chinese decided you were to be liquidated. The Russians decided they wanted to know what you knew about Kung. In the general mix-up, Nurse Roche got shot instead of you. Right now, we have given out you are dead. We have a few days free from pressure before the Chinese and the Russians get to know you are still alive, then they will come after you again."

She stared down at her long, shapely hands, her face expressionless, then she said, "So that's it. Well, I know nothing about Kung. Absolutely nothing."

"Why did you leave him?"

"He bored me."

"Then why should they want to kill you?"

She hesitated, then still not looking at him, she said,

"Kung is possessive. I was his toy. He breaks his toys if they don't give him pleasure."

"A young girl died because of you," Girland said quietly.

"You might have died, but she was the unlucky one. Your chances of survival are still pretty thin. You may think you can play this on your own, but I assure you you can't. I have only to walk out on you for you to be in real trouble. You have no money. You have no passport. You will be in a hell of a jam unless you co-operate."

She looked steadily at him. "What does that mean?"

"You must know something about Kung. Every scrap of information we can get about him could be useful."

"I can tell you about his sex life if that would interest you," she said, shrugging.

"That is all I know about him. I had a house of my own. He visited me twice a week. He never talked about his work. He was generous, a little kinky and very dull."

"Kinky?"

"He had this tattoo mania." She leaned back in her chair and stared out of the open window.

"I hadn't much money. I was secretary to a Swedish businessman who was trying to sell lumber to the Chinese. He paid me badly. I met Kung and he offered me three hundred dollars a week to be his mistress."

She shrugged. "A house, servants and a car went with the offer. I accepted. It pleased him to put his stamp on me ... so I let him."

"Did you ever visit his home?"

"I went once. It wasn't a home, it was a museum."

"So he bored you and you left him," Girland said. "He must have been very boring for you to give up three hundred dollars a week."

"He was."

"And he was so annoyed, he told his agents to kill you?"

"Yes."

"How were you planning to live after the luxury of a house, servants and a car, plus three hundred dollars a week?"

She shrugged. "I can always get a job."

"That's not very convincing." Girland's voice hardened. "Kung owns one of the finest collections of jewellery and jade in the world. You didn't pick up some trifle before you left, planning to sell it and retire in comfort for the rest of your life?"

Erica stiffened for a brief moment, then she relaxed and smiled mockingly at him.

"Are you suggesting I am a thief?"

"Oh no, an opportunist, perhaps." He regarded her. "Like myself."

"You are beginning to interest me," she said. "So you are an opportunist." She studied him, then nodded. "You certainly look like one. Just who are you?"

"I won't bore you with my biography. I am an opportunist. I search for a rainbow in every sky. Right now, I have to admit, it hasn't got me anywhere."

Girland made a rueful grimace. "I work for the Central Intelligence Agency because the work offers me excitement, interest and money. When I am not working for them, I try to earn a living as a street photographer. But like you, I am bored with my way of life. I am looking for a big killing."

"I think I would like a cigarette," she said.

When he had given her one and lit it, she stared out of the window and he could see she was thinking.

As she said nothing for a minute or so, Girland said, "We

are leaving here. We are going to stay in an apartment owned by a dealer in precious stones. He is also an opportunist. He has several rich contacts. He handles items without asking questions and he pays cash."

She slowly turned her head and stared thoughtfully at him. "Does he?"

Girland smiled at her. "Think it over. If my boss is convinced you know nothing about Kung except the way he behaves in bed, he will drop you like a hot potato. Then you will be out on a limb. Your chums at the Chinese Embassy will come after you and you will end up like poor little Ginny with a hole in your head."

"Do you think so?" She was very calm and her eyes mocking.

"Let's leave it for now. You have a few days to think it over. Here is a beautiful wig. I'll get Ginny's uniform. We leave here in half an hour."

When he had left the room, Erica Olsen stared out of the window, her slim fingers tapping gently on her knee.

The apartment was spacious, luxuriously furnished and had a magnificent view of the harbour, Onassis' yacht, the Palace and the Casino.

There was a big terrace with sun umbrellas, furniture, tubs crammed with begonias and geraniums and an orange tree heavy with fruit.

Erica stood on the terrace, her hands on the balcony rail and looked down at the view.

Girland said, "You settle in. I'm going down to organise dinner. I don't think it would be wise for you to go out just yet."

She didn't say anything, but continued to stare down at the view.

Her face was thoughtful.

Girland had the idea she was wrestling with a problem.

Leaving the apartment, he found a nearby *Traiteur* and ordered smoked salmon, *coq au vin*, forest strawberries and a carton of ice-cream to be sent up to the apartment in a couple of hours' time.

It gave him some pleasure to pay for the meal with Dorey's money.

He thought regretfully that he was going to miss this luxury when eventually he returned to Paris, but cheered himself up with the reminder that with any luck he might return a rich man.

Deciding to give Erica plenty of time to think, he drove to the Casino.

He spent an hour there and lost thirty francs, then he drove back, took the elevator to the top floor of the building and entered Yew's apartment.

Erica was sitting in the sun, a cigarette smouldering between her fingers.

She had changed out of the Nurse's uniform and was now wearing a white and blue dress that fitted her full, sensual curves.

She didn't look towards him, and seeing she was still preoccupied with her thoughts, he went into his bedroom, stripped off and took a cold shower.

By the time he had shaved and changed, he heard her moving around in her bedroom which was opposite his.

"Dinner will be along in ten minutes," he called and began to set the table on the terrace.

A little after 8.30 p.m. a boy delivered the meal and Girland, humming under his breath, set the food out on Yew's beautiful Chinese plates.

He was drawing the cork from a bottle of Margaux '45

when Erica came out onto the terrace. She now seemed much more relaxed.

"This looks good," she said as Girland drew out her chair. She smiled up at him. "You are very well organised, aren't you?"

"When I have other people's money to spend," Girland said, sitting opposite her, "I'm right on the ball."

He poured a shot of vodka into two crystal glasses to go with the smoked salmon. "I'm not so hot when it comes to looking after my own money. I am better handling other people's headaches than my own."

"I'm not good either about handling my affairs." She ate some salmon. "This is delicious."

"That's why I thought you and I could get together." Girland passed a plate of brown bread and butter.

"Tell me how you managed to get hold of Kung's black pearl."

She cut a piece of salmon, regarded it, then put it in her mouth.

Watching her, Girland saw her face was expressionless. "Is this Scotch or Norwegian salmon?" she asked.

He laughed. "Scotch."

"It is the best." She sipped her vodka, then looked straight into his eyes. "This friend of yours with rich contacts. If he had the pearl, could he sell it?"

"Yes. The sale would be arranged very discreetly. There are still a number of collectors with lots of money who can't resist anything really unique and who are prepared to buy and not ask questions."

"Is that right?"

She ate in silence and Girland, patient, enjoyed the salmon while waiting for her next move.

When they had finished, he removed the plates and

served the *coq au vin* that was standing on the electric hot plate.

"I am sure my friend won't mind us drinking his best wine on such an occasion," he said as he poured the Margaux. "This is a beauty."

"Did your friend mention a price?" she asked after sampling the *coq au vin* and praising it.

"He would try for three million dollars. That would be gross, of course. He would have to have a cut."

Girland gave her his charming smile. "I would have to have one too."

"What would be the price net then?"

"Two million which, of course, is a nice, useful sum."

She regarded him thoughtfully, then nodded.

"I suppose it is."

"But you were hoping for more?"

"One always does." She laid down her knife and fork. "That was really very good. The wine is wonderful."

"One should always eat well when arranging a deal."

"Is that what we are doing?"

"I was under that impression."

As she said nothing, he cleared the plates and put the strawberries on the table and the ice-cream in one of Yew's precious egg shell Chinese bowls.

She said suddenly, "There is always the possibility that he wouldn't get three million dollars."

"He seems pretty confident that he will get it."

"The transaction would be in cash?"

"That would be a lot of cash. He could arrange to pay in Swiss bearer bonds. These are as good as cash and much more convenient to handle. That's the way I would take my share."

"You seem very sure you are going to have a share," she

said as she helped herself to ice-cream.

"I'm not only an opportunist," Girland said. "I am also an optimist."

"Just how would the deal be handled?"

"Yew would have to see the pearl. He would have to satisfy himself it was Kung's pearl and not a clever fake. He would then contact the buyer. There would be a minor delay, then the bonds would be handed over and that would be that."

"It sounds very simple, doesn't it?"

"Where is the pearl, Erica?"

"I was wondering when you were going to ask that. It is quite safe."

She leaned back in her chair and gave him an amused smile. "So you see ... I admit I have the pearl."

Girland drew in a long breath of relief. His hunch had paid off, he thought, now for the deal.

He and Yew would split the million dollars, and at long last he would be in the money.

"I had an idea you had it. Well, now, when can you show it to Yew?"

"His offer is absurd," Erica said calmly. "The pearl is utterly unique. There is no other like it in the world. I have already been offered four million and I want six."

Girland stared at her. "But there's not that amount of money in the hands of any collector," he said. "Now, look, Erica ..."

"I have a contact who says there could be. There is a certain oil man who is supposed to be worth two hundred million dollars and he is a collector. He could afford to pay six million for it."

"Then why don't you sell it to him?" Girland asked, sure she was lying.

"There are complications."

"What complications?"

"That is not your affair."

Girland finished his strawberries, then getting up, he poured coffee from the percolator.

"Let's sit comfortably and enjoy the view," he said and carried the two cups of coffee to a side table and dropped into one of the lounging chairs.

Erica joined him. They both looked down at the glittering lights round the harbour and the Palace.

"Tell me about the complications."

"That is not your affair," she repeated, lighting a cigarette. "Will your Mr Yew go to six million?"

"I don't think so." Girland sipped his coffee, then said, "You've talked yourself into a tough spot, baby. You now can't do without me. Two heads are better than one. I'm good at complications. Tell me about them."

"You are mistaken," she said quietly. "I can do without you, and I don't understand what you mean when you say I am in a tough spot, and please don't call me baby. I don't like it."

"I'm sorry, it won't occur again," Girland said, smiling. "Forgive me. Let me explain why you can't do without me. You have admitted you have the pearl. In crude language, you have stolen it. Now if you and I can't co-operate, there is nothing to stop me giving this information to the press. Erica Olsen, mistress of Feng Hoh Kung, has stolen the famous Black Grape and is in hiding. What a story! I could then telephone Dorey and tell him the only information you have about Kung is his behaviour in bed. Dorey will immediately withdraw his support and protection. He is a mean man and hates to spend a dollar if he gets no return. In the meantime, every collector, no matter how much he would like to own the pearl, will shun it. It will have become as hot as a red-hot stove. It is only if there is no publicity and the deal is done in secret that you can hope to sell the pearl. Then the French police will arrest you. You will probably languish in jail for six months or even longer until they are satisfied you can't or won't tell them where you have hidden the pearl.

"You mustn't overlook the fact that the French Government are trying to get on friendly terms with the Chinese. Maybe the police will persuade you to talk, but if they don't, then they will eventually get bored with you and turn you loose. You will walk out of prison into the arms of Kung's hatchet men. They will either slit your pretty throat or else they will persuade you to talk, and make no mistake about it a Chinese thug can make anyone talk. So, being intelligent, you will see by now, you can't do without me. I think three million dollars for nothing isn't a bad rake off. If your complications are really so complicated, then I would advise you to take the three million. I might add that I don't believe anyone would pay six million for the pearl and that you are bluffing. Do you get the picture?"

If he had expected to disconcert her, he was disappointed.

She let her head drop back on the padded cushion of the lounging chair and she laughed.

"I am beginning to think you are the man I have been looking for," she said.

"You seem to be as unscrupulous as I am. You could have yourself a deal."

"Where is the pearl, Erica?"

"I wish I could trust you." She looked steadily at him. "There is so much involved. I can't make up my mind about you."

Girland got to his feet.

"Let us get to know each other better," he said. "There is no better place for a man and a woman to do that than in a bed."

Her eyes widened with surprise. "Do you think going to bed with you will solve my problem?"

Girland reached down, took her hand and pulled her to her feet.

"I don't know. Frankly, I don't much care. I know you are beautiful and I want you. I think we have talked enough for tonight. I think now we should make love and forget about business. Then tomorrow, when we know each other better, we can talk again. What do you think?"

She rested her hands on his shoulders and she studied his face. "You are an extraordinary man."

"I suppose I am."

He put his arms around her and drew her to him.

She yielded.

His hands slid down her back, cupped her buttocks and he pulled her hard against him, his mouth searching for hers.

She shook her head. "No, wait. Let's go to my room." She broke free, smiling. "I don't do this with every man I meet, but I do now want to know you better."

"It's the certain way," Girland said and he walked with her across the big lounge, down the wide passage and to her bedroom door.

He pushed open the door and as they moved into the room, she gave him a hard shove that sent him off balance, and slid away from him.

The man standing by the open window, a silenced 7.65 mm Luger automatic in his hand, gave Girland the biggest shock of his life.

8

The man didn't look particularly dangerous, but any man holding a Luger equipped with a silencer, was unpredictable and Girland was careful to make no sudden move.

"Come right in, Mr Girland," the man said. "I have been looking forward to meeting you."

Girland studied him. He was tall, fattish, balding with a pronounced paunch. He would be around sixty years of age. His blue eyes, his broad features, his wide fixed smile revealing glittering white dentures, his immaculate lightweight suit and his expensive French tie gave him a solid and substantial personality. Girland saw he handled the gun expertly as if the gun was as familiar to him as his aftershave lotion. With his sharp perception, Girland decided this man was a smooth trickster, probably without funds, but dressing the part of a rich man to obtain credit from snob shopkeepers who couldn't fail to be impressed by his appearance.

"How did you get in here?" Girland asked as he moved into the large airy bedroom.

"Carlota let me in while you were ordering that excellent dinner."

"Carlota?"

Erica was now sitting on the bed. She looked faintly amused as she watched Girland walk over to the stool before the dressing-table and sit on it.

"Mr Girland," the fat man said, leaning against the wall, "before we go any further, please don't try anything heroic. I am an expert shot and I can, at this range, blow your right knee cap to pieces should you decide to be difficult. Since you are a very active man, I am sure you wouldn't like that to happen."

"Okay," Girland said, and lifted his hands in mock surrender. "You have made your point. Is she Carlota? I was under the impression she was Erica Olsen."

"She is Carlota Olsen ... Erica's sister. These two very handsome girls are my daughters," the fat man said, beaming at Carlota. "Mr Girland, I have been eavesdropping. I have been quite carried away by your persuasive sales talk. I have reached the conclusion that you are exactly the man we have been looking for. I think Carlota is of the same mind." He looked at his daughter. "Aren't you, my dear?"

"Oh, yes," she said. "I think he could do very well."

Without taking his eyes off Girland, the fat man bent to pick up a portable tape recorder that had been concealed behind a chair.

"Mr Girland," he said, "I have a perfect recording of your talk with my daughter. You were threatening to blackmail her. I am now in the happy position to be able to blackmail you. This small reel of tape would interest Mr Dorey. I doubt very much if it would please him. I am under the impression that if he should ever listen to your recorded remarks, he would make life extremely unpleasant for you."

Girland laughed. His amusement was so genuine that the fat man joined in while Carlota regarded them with an impatient frown.

"When you have finished amusing yourselves," she said tartly, "suppose we get down to business?"

Girland ignored her.

"Your trick," he said to the fat man. "Your name's Olsen? Right?"

"Erich Olsen."

Girland took a packet of cigarettes from his pocket.

"This fascinates me. Suppose you fill me in?"

"You do agree that the tape could embarrass you?"

"Of course. It wouldn't do you any good either, but let's skip that. Tell me what's cooking."

"My daughters and I," Olsen said, "are like you, Mr Girland. We are opportunists. We have been on the lookout for a big killing. We have been extremely patient and now we are in sight of our goal.

"Erica, who is a year older than Carlota, had a position as a badly paid secretary. She went with her boss on a trade mission to Peking. There she met Feng Hoh Kung. Now, Erica is extremely attractive. Kung made a proposal and Erica accepted. This was quite a blow to Carlota and myself. We felt our little trio had broken up. However, Erica hadn't forgotten us. After some months, she decided the life she had chosen wasn't for her. She also discovered it was going to be very difficult for her to leave Peking. However, she was fortunate enough to meet a Chinese youth who was to prove helpful. It was he who got her out of China. At this time, Carlota was in Stockholm." Olsen flashed his white dentures at Girland. "I was in Paris. There was a little misunderstanding with the Swedish police, and it was wiser for me to live in Paris." He shrugged. "You know how these things can happen. Carlota received a cable from her sister, asking her to come at once to Hong Kong. There was a hint in the cable that it would be worth Carlota's time and trouble if she did so. She consulted me and I advised her to go. Erica had found Kung a disagreeable old gentleman and to compensate her for the various experiences she had been subjected to, she took with her when she left, the famous Black Grape pearl." Again the white dentures flashed. "She was quickly missed and Kung's agents were alerted in Hong Kong. Erica found herself in a trap and she was forced into hiding. She and Carlota conceived the idea that Carlota should impersonate Erica and draw off the hunt. It was a very brave thing to do. Erica's Chinese boyfriend found a tattooist who copied the well known Kung's initials on Carlota and she returned to Paris. Erica had given her a Chinese drug that temporarily blots out the memory. We needed publicity and we wanted Kung to believe that Erica had reached Paris. Carlota took the drug. This was necessary as we knew that under examination – if she hadn't taken the drug – she would be found to be faking and that, of course, would have led to complications. By the oddest chance, this unfortunate nurse was shot instead of Carlota. Fortunately for us, you had the idea of telling the press that it was Erica who had died. Now the pressure is off, but there are still a number of difficulties. We need your help, Mr Girland. Would you have any objection to going to Hong Kong and bringing back the pearl?"

Girland stared at him.

"Why don't you go?"

Olsen smiled.

"I am in a slightly unfortunate position. I am safe enough living in France, but in British territory, I could be embarrassed. It wouldn't be wise for me to leave the country at the moment."

"Let's get this straight. You want me to go to Hong Kong, collect the pearl, bring it back here and fix the deal with Yew at three million dollars? Is that right?"

"You will also bring Erica with you. She wouldn't part with the pearl to a stranger, Mr Girland."

"Why doesn't she just come? Now the pressure's off, she could come, couldn't she?"

"Well, no. It hasn't been possible to get her a false passport. It is believed that at least two of the men at the police control are in Kung's pay. I had hoped with your connections that you might get her a false passport."

"Is she like you in appearance?" Girland asked Carlota.

"Yes, very much like me."

"Dorey gave me a passport and also a marriage certificate in case you needed convincing that I was your husband. I still have both documents. I see no reason why Erica couldn't travel on this passport."

Olsen beamed.

"You see, Mr Girland, how wise we were asking for your help."

"This will cost money," Girland said after a moment of thought. "Have you got any?"

Olsen shook his head.

"Money is something I seldom have, but it did occur to me that your friend Mr Yew might be persuaded to finance the trip to Hong Kong."

Girland laughed.

"You certainly are an opportunist. Yes, I should think if he were definitely promised the pearl, he would advance the necessary cash. I'll talk to him."

"Then there's Carlota," Olsen said. "I imagine the French police won't let her out of France until they are convinced that she has had nothing to do with Kung. Carlota should return to Stockholm. There are rather pressing affairs for her to attend to. Can you help her to leave quickly, Mr Girland?"

"Shouldn't be difficult." Girland turned to Carlota. "You will have to see Dorey. He may keep you a few days asking all kinds of questions, but if we have our story set up, you should be free to travel by the end of the week."

"Well, then ..." Olsen pushed himself away from the wall. "We seem to have had a very useful meeting, Mr Girland. The sooner we get Erica back the better. What will your first move be?"

"I'll see Yew and raise some money. Tomorrow morning, Carlota and I will fly to Paris. I will talk to Dorey, leave her with him and get off to Hong Kong. Where do I find Erica?"

"Carlota will give you the address."

Girland turned on his charm.

"Now we are partners, Olsen, let me have the tape." He got to his feet, but paused as Olsen lifted the gun and pointed it at him. With a flash of his dentures, Olsen said, "I'm sorry, Mr Girland, but I am keeping the tape as insurance. You are far too great an opportunist for me to trust you entirely. Although it would be difficult for you to get the pearl away from Erica, it would not be impossible, and from what I have seen of you, you can achieve the impossible. So long as I keep the tape, then I feel fairly certain of getting my money. If by any chance you attempt a double cross, I will not only send the tape to Dorey, but I will send a copy to the Press Association. I will make absolutely sure no one will benefit from the pearl except the Olsen family."

Girland grinned.

"It was worth a try," he said. He looked at Carlota who was watching him. "Your father deserves to prosper, doesn't he?"

"He hasn't up to now," Carlota said. "But he keeps trying."

"Excuse me for not shaking hands, Mr Girland," Olsen said, waving the gun apologetically. "I will be expecting a telephone call from you. Carlota will give you the number."

He walked around Girland, carrying the tape recorder in his left hand, the gun pointing at Girland.

"So long," Girland said.

The bedroom door closed, then the front door slammed and Girland looked at Carlota with a quizzical smile. "You are quite a family. I can't wait to meet Erica."

"She isn't as nice as I am," Carlota said. "She is prettier, but she hasn't my charm."

"That is sad for her." Girland looked at his watch. "I wonder if I can get hold of Yew. It's getting late, but he might be in. My life seems to be spent haggling about money."

He crossed the room and opened the door.

Carlota said, "Haven't you forgotten something?"

He turned and looked at her, raising his eyebrows.

"Have I?"

"I thought we had come in here to get to know each other better."

Girland laughed.

"I must be getting old." He closed the door. "I can talk to Yew tomorrow morning."

Staring at him, her violet-blue eyes dark and inviting, Carlota slowly zipped open her dress.

Mavis Paul, Dorey's new secretary was dark, beautifully built and very assured. She had fought her way up to this position from the typist pool. She was efficient, pretty, diamond hard and determined to make good. She regarded Girland unfavourably as he wandered into her office. This sloppily dressed man in an open neck sports shirt and faded blue jeans made her hackles rise. This was no way for an American to dress in Paris, she thought as she regarded him with a cold, hostile stare.

"Well?" she snapped.

"Apart from a slight hangover, I'm not too bad, thank you," Girland said. He placed his large sun-tanned hands on the desk and leaned towards her, smiling. "You must be the new recruit. Ever get lonely, baby? I take care of all the lonely chicks in Paris."

Mavis stiffened.

"How ..."

"... dare you make such a remark," Girland broke in, beating her to it. "Sorry. You are so lovely and you have lonely eyes. How's the old square? Is he busy?"

Mavis looked helplessly around the office, but there was no one to help her cope with this man who was smiling at her, and she had to admit he did have a charming smile.

"Mr Dorey is busy right now," she managed to say and then was horrified when Girland reached over her desk, flicked down the switch that connected the desk intercom with Dorey's office and said in a loud, sinister sounding voice, "The Russians have landed. I advise immediate surrender."

She sat petrified. Then Dorey's cold, dry voice came out of the intercom box. "Is that you, Girland? Come in."

"See? Simple," Girland said as he flicked up the switch. He leaned forward and kissed Mavis on her cheek. "Let's have a date, baby." He took her solid slap on his face without flinching. He straightened, felt his jaw and grimaced.

"Phew! That could have laid Clay on the canvas. You pack a mean punch, honey."

"Get in there before I throw my typewriter at you!" Mavis said furiously.

"Did anyone tell you that when you are in a rage, sparks fly out of your eyes?" Girland asked, moving away from the desk. "Sparks like brilliant little stars. Quite the most attractive phenomenon I have ever seen from any woman." He blew her a kiss. "Bye for now and don't pine for me. We're sure to meet again." He crossed the room and entered Dorey's office.

Dorey, behind his desk, glared suspiciously at him as he came in.

"What's happened? Why are you in Paris? Don't tell me you've lost her again!"

"Oh no." Girland sat down and reached for one of Dorey's expensive cigarettes in the box on the desk. "Nothing like that."

"What's happened to your face?" Dorey said, staring at the bright red mark on Girland's cheek.

"Collision with an irresistible force," Girland explained and laughed. "It's an occupational hazard."

"You haven't been interfering with my secretary, have you?" Dorey asked, frowning at Girland.

"No ... actually she interfered with me." Girland lit his cigarette, then went on, "Dorey, prepare for the worst. We have laid an addled egg."

Dorey stiffened.

"What does that mean?"

"Just that ... the egg is addled." Girland made himself more comfortable. "Our subject has her memory back, and guess what? She isn't Erica Olsen. She is Carlota Olsen, Erica's sister. How do you like that? From what she tells me, she was the smoke screen behind which Erica could disappear. As Carlota will tell you, Erica got bored with Kung and ran off. She managed to reach Hong Kong, but Kung's agents, breathing fire, caught up with her. She had to go into hiding. She persuaded her sister to come out to Hong Kong and then talked her into impersonating her. A tattooist faked Kung's initials on Carlota's *derrière* and then Carlota returned to Paris. She took some drug that wiped out her memory and she was then planted for you and the gendarmes to find. While the Chinese were trying to knock her off and the Russians trying to kidnap her, Erica got out of Hong Kong and has got lost. Just where she is is anyone's guess. Carlota has no idea. So that's the sad story."

Dorey leaned back in his chair. His thin lips tightened.

"Where is this woman?"

"Carlota? Right outside. I told her you would want to talk to her. She's ready to co-operate. She did this to help her sister. She had no idea that there were any political implications. She was just giving her sister time to get away from Kung." Girland shook his head. "Quite a brave thing for a girl to have done."

"I'll talk to her," Dorey said grimly.

"I'll shoo her in." Girland got to his feet. "Well, I guess this lets me out, doesn't it? I'm sorry it didn't work out the way you hoped it would. I did what you wanted ... it's just one of those things." He smiled at Dorey. "Let me see now, you owe me ten thousand francs ... right?"

"Wrong!" Dorey snapped. "I gave you twenty thousand francs. So you owe me ten thousand francs and I'm going to have it!"

Girland looked sad.

"You have no idea what it cost me to rent an apartment in Monte Carlo. Then there was the fare up for the two of us. As Carlota was a little nervous, I thought we had better travel first-class. Anyway, I'll let you have an account. I think you will find you owe me rather than I owe you. Anyway, you talk to Carlota." Girland's smile widened. "You'll like her ... she's quite a girl."

"I want that passport back, Girland." Girland stared blankly at him.

"What passport?"

"The passport I had faked for this woman."

"Of course." Girland clapped his hand to his forehead. "I remember. Well, for Pete's sake, I'm getting forgetful. I left it in the right-hand top drawer of your desk in your villa. I'm sorry ... I should have brought it with me ... clean went out of my mind."

"It's all right. I'll get Diallo to mail it to me." Dorey regarded Girland thoughtfully. "I have an idea you are up to something. What are you going to do now?"

"I might take a little vacation. I have saved a little money and before returning to my job, I think I deserve a vacation."

Dorey wasn't fooled for a moment.

"Listen to me, Girland, if I find you have been untrustworthy, I'll make it my business to fix you, and believe me, I could fix you."

Girland looked innocently at him.

"That's not very friendly. Just because you get landed with an addled egg, Dorey, you can't blame me ... now can you?"

"Just remember what I've said. I don't think I am going to employ you again. Whenever you have an assignment it goes wrong, but somehow you benefit."

"Just chance," Girland said, moving to the door. "You might still need me, Dorey, old pal. If I can put up with you,

I can't see why you can't be big-minded and put up with me. Bye now," and he went out of the office.

Mavis Paul was typing, making the machine sound like a quick-fire machine gun. She didn't look up nor pause as Girland came to rest by her desk.

Girland studied the little plaque bearing her name that stood on her desk. He picked up a scratch pad and pen and wrote the name down.

"Pretty name ... pretty girl," he murmured. He put the slip of paper into his shirt pocket and went out into the ante-room where Carlota was waiting.

"Go on in," he said. "He'll talk a lot, but the foundation is laid for you. I'll get off. See you sometime soon."

They touched hands, smiled at each other, then Girland went down to where he had parked his Fiat 600.

The following morning Girland, arrived by taxi at Orly airport to catch the 9 a.m. flight via Rome to Hong Kong. He was carrying a lightweight suitcase and he wore a well worn, slightly crumpled tropical blue suit. He handed his suitcase to an elderly porter, and followed him to the Air France reception desk. He tipped the porter and paid the airport dues. He was told his flight was AF 632 and, there might be a slight delay in Rome.

Jean Redoun, the porter, listened long enough to register these facts, then he walked quickly to the nearest telephone booth. He remembered Girland by his photograph, and he knew the Soviet Embassy was more than interested in him. He put through a call and spoke briefly to Kovski.

After the call, Kovski sat for a long moment, frowning into space. Malik, somewhat in disgrace, had been sent to Rome to check on a British agent who seemed ready to defect. Why was Girland going to Hong Kong? Kovski asked himself. The woman was dead. They were certain of that. Then why Hong Kong? He didn't hesitate for more than a few seconds. He reached for the telephone and called Rome.

Girland believed in luxury at other people's expense. He had decided to travel first class, but he did have some difficulty in persuading Jacques Yew to advance the fare. Yew couldn't see what was wrong with travelling economy class, but eventually Girland talked him out of this way of thinking.

Girland enjoyed the trip. The first-class section on the aircraft wasn't crowded, and the air hostess, a pretty little thing with a lively smile and flirtatious eyes didn't hold his shabby suit against him. She thought he could be an eccentric millionaire, and besides, he had a charming smile. She was continually pampering him with caviar, champagne and snacks.

At Rome, Girland left the aircraft and had two quick double Scotches in the airport bar. He stretched his legs, bought the latest Hadley Chase paperback and returned to the aircraft.

Three minutes before the aircraft took off, Malik, slightly out of breath, hurried across the tarmac and climbed the stairs into the economy-class compartment. As he fastened his safety belt, he congratulated himself on the speed of his driving and his luck to find an empty seat on the plane.

Kovski had been very emphatic. Malik was not to lose Girland. Girland would not be travelling to Hong Kong unless Erica Olsen had given him some important information before she had died. That, Kovski felt was certain. The Soviet Security wanted this information. Malik's instructions were to get it at all cost. The Soviet Agents in Hong Kong had been alerted. They would work under Malik. This was Malik's opportunity to make good his failure.

Malik had sneered to himself, but he had made frantic efforts to get on the plane, and by three minutes to spare, he had succeeded.

While he and Girland were being shot through space towards Hong Kong, Yet-Sen at the Paris Chinese Embassy was making a report in code that was to be cabled to Peking. Yet-Sen was satisfied with himself. Admittedly, he had lost three promising agents, but after all, agents were expendable. The point was he had carried out his instructions. The woman was dead.

As an afterthought, he added a description of Girland to his report.

"This man," he wrote, "is dangerous and should be in our files. A photograph and details of his method of operations will follow in the diplomatic bag."

This cable arrived in Peking eighteen hours before Girland landed in Hong Kong. A warning about Girland, with his description, was flashed to every airport in Asia. Not that they were expecting Girland, but the Chinese are thorough and it was part of their system to take no chances.

So without being aware of it, Girland was heading for a wasps' nest. He not only had Malik on his plane, but now a certain Chinese Customs official at the Kai Tak airport had his description.

Eating an excellent sauté of chicken, washed down with a very presentable Bordeaux wine, Girland at that moment hadn't a care in the world. He was heading towards riches, and about to arrive at the foot of his rainbow.

Girland was no stranger to Hong Kong. This, he thought as he walked out of the airport into the blistering sunshine, would be his fourth visit. Once he had met a young, American heiress on a world tour. She had insisted that he should be her bodyguard. Since her body was exceptionally inviting, Girland had raised no objections. They had spent four exciting and somewhat erotic weeks in Hong Kong. Later, he had been assigned by the CIA to help to break up an opium ring and Hong Kong had been the centre of operations. He and Harry Curtis, the resident Agent, had spent days in a police boat and Girland had got to know the various outer islands around Taipang Wan, Tathong and in the East Lamma Channel.

Curtis was the last person Girland wanted to run into at this moment, and knowing Curtis had the habit of meeting aircraft from Europe, he kept a sharp eye out for him. He was so occupied watching for Curtis' burly figure that he failed to notice Malik trailing along behind him.

The Chinese Customs officer at the barrier studied Girland's passport and then looked thoughtfully at him. Then he returned the passport, saluted and motioned Girland through the barrier. As soon as Girland began walking towards a row of taxis, the Customs officer jerked his thumb in his direction and a fat Chinese, wearing a well-worn black business suit, went after Girland.

All this wasn't lost on Malik whose sharp eyes had seen the signal and the fat Chinese wander after Girland. Malik glanced around.

Branska, the resident Soviet agent, came out of the crowd and shook Malik's hand. Branska was a short, heavily-built man with sandy, thinning hair and freckles.

"It's all right," he said. "He's taken care of. I have three men covering him. Let's go to the hotel. We'll get a report as soon as they find out where he is going."

Malik nodded and the two men walked over to a waiting car.

Girland told the taxi driver to take him to the Star Ferry. He relaxed back in the cab as it rushed him along the crowded waterfront with its hordes of trotting coolies, carrying enormous burdens, slung on bamboo poles, the rickshaws, the overladen trucks, the big American cars driven by sleek rich-looking Chinese, bicycles making suicidal dashes through the traffic and every now and then a lovely Chinese girl, her cheongsam slit to four inches above her knees, in a rickshaw, her legs crossed, her hands demurely in her lap.

Girland loved Hong Kong. This was a town, he thought, teeming with life and energy where anything could happen and where money could be made.

He paid off the taxi at the ferry, then passing through the turnstile, he got on board the waiting boat.

Two of Malik's agents and the fat Chinese also got on the boat.

Ten minutes later, Girland left the boat station on the Hong Kong side and took a taxi to a small hotel on the Wanchai waterfront where he had stayed previously.

By this time he had become aware that he was being followed. Girland had a strongly developed sense of self-preservation. He had quickly spotted Malik's agents during the crossing, but he had failed to spot the fat Chinese who was sitting near him, reading the *Hong Kong Times*.

As Girland paid off his taxi, he saw a car drive past. The two thick-set men were in the car and they looked studiously away from him as the car went on up the waterfront.

Girland grinned. Well, he would have to be careful, he told himself. He paid no attention to a fat Chinese in a shabby black suit who was standing near him, buying a pack of cigarettes from a street vendor. Girland climbed the steep steps to the hotel lobby. He was greeted with a wide smile of welcome by an elderly Chinese with a wispy beard. Wan See had been the owner of the hotel for many years and he had an excellent memory for faces.

After greeting him, Girland went up more stairs to a small clean room that overlooked the waterfront. He took a shower, changed into a sports shirt and jeans, and then went down to Wan See.

The owner of the hotel was in the pay of the American Embassy and he could be relied on. Girland warned him that he was on official business and he must be careful no one got into his room while he was out.

Wan See had housed a number of American Agents over the years and he knew his business.

"That is okay," he said. "No one comes here unless I know him."

"I have a telephone call to make."

Wan See waved to a booth.

Carlota had given Girland a telephone number to call when he arrived. This number, she had explained was to a villa on the Peak where Erica was in hiding. He dialled the number and waited.

There was a brief delay, then a man's voice said, "Who is that, please?"

"A friend who comes from Paris," Girland said, using the phrase Carlota had given him.

He heard a quick hiss of breath.

"I hope you had a good journey." This was the counter password Carlota had given him and Girland relaxed.

"Well, I'm here. I am at the Lotus Hotel, Wanchai. Do I come to you or will you come to me?"

"It would be better if you come to me," the man said. "The situation is difficult. It is safer not to talk now. I will send a woman to bring you to me. She will be wearing a red cheongsam and a diamond in her left ear."

"She sounds charming," Girland said as the line went dead.

He again consulted Wan See.

"There is a girl coming. The hotel is being watched. She and I will be leaving and it is important we won't be followed."

Wan See giggled.

"There is no trouble. Every half-hour girls come here. The lower rooms are rented for love. There is a staircase to the roof. You can leave that way. You cross two roofs, descend by a fire escape to an alley that leads to the waterfront."

Girland returned to his room and waited. He thought longingly of an air conditioner as the heat flowed through the open window, turning the small room into an oven.

An hour and five minutes later, there came a tap on the door.

Girland got off the bed and opened the door. A slim Chinese girl, wearing a scarlet cheongsam, a diamond sparkling in her left ear lobe, smiled at him.

"You expect me?"

Girland liked Chinese girls. During his previous stays in Hong Kong he had slept with a number of them. They had technique and they took lovemaking seriously. This girl was not only pretty: she was sensationally sensuous.

"Who are you?" he asked, moving back so she could come in.

"My name is Tan-Toy. I work along the waterfront. I make professional love."

"You do?" Girland laughed. "That is something we might discuss later. Right now, let's go."

They climbed the staircase to the roof and moving cautiously, they crossed two other roofs and descended by the iron fire escape into the alley below.

They were watched by one of Malik's agents who knew all about Wan See's escape route. He had been posted on a nearby roof for the past two hours. Using a walkie-talkie, he alerted Malik that Girland with a Chinese woman was leaving his hotel.

The fat Chinese had seen Tan-Toy arrive at the hotel. He knew about the villa on the Peak and had been watching it now for three or four days. He also alerted his men by short wave radio that Girland might be heading towards the villa.

There was a considerable amount of traffic going up to the Peak and as Tan-Toy drove Girland in an Austin Cooper up the winding road, he kept looking back to see if they were being followed.

She said, "It is all right. The lady is not there any longer. It is Hung Yan you are going to see."

"Is he the guy I spoke to on the telephone?"

"Yes."

"If she's not there, where is she?"

"I don't know." Tan-Toy gave him a flashing smile.

"Who are you? How do you get muddled up in this?"

"Hung Yan is my friend. He helped me once when I was ill. I like to help people when they help me."

Eventually the car pulled up outside a small, dark villa, perched on the edge of the mountain with a fine view of Hong Kong and distant Kowloon.

"Go right in," the girl said as Girland got out of the car. "When you have finished your business, we might meet."

"Where do I find you?" Girland asked, bending down to look at her through the car window.

"Wan See knows ... ask him." She waved her hand, looked again into his eyes, then reversing the car, she drove away.

Girland looked down the long dark winding road, watching the red tail lights of her car disappear. No other car moved on the road.

He walked quickly down a path that led to the villa and rang the bell. The front door immediately opened.

"Please come in."

A shadowy figure let him into a small, stiflingly hot room lit by a small table lamp.

The two men looked at each other. Hung Yan was a slightly built, young Chinese wearing a black, baggy, Chinese coat and trousers. His glittering eyes were feverish and when he shook hands, his skin felt dry and hot.

Girland introduced himself.

"The situation is very bad," Hung Yan said. "They know I am here. I don't think they can make up their minds whether she is dead or alive. Otherwise they would have got rid of me before now. Have you a passport for her? That is what she wants."

"I have it. Where is she?"

"I will take you to her. She is on a junk, anchored off Pak Kok."

"How do you come to be here?" Girland asked curiously.

"This villa belongs to my father who is in America. I brought Erica here a week ago, but she didn't feel safe. She is very frightened. The junk belongs to my cousin's fishing fleet. It is old and he is not using it. Erica thought she would be safer there than here."

"Is she alone?"

"Yes, she is alone and frightened. I am sorry for her." Hung Yan made a helpless movement with his hands. "We are in love. She is in a very dangerous situation and it worries me very much."

"I'm not absolutely sure I haven't been followed," Girland said. "When do we go?"

Hung Yan shrugged.

"It doesn't matter. They know I am here. They hope I will lead them to her." He went to a cupboard. Opening it, he took from it two long knives in leather scabbards. "Can you use a knife? It is better than a gun."

"Oh, sure," Girland said. He took the knife from Hung Yan, pulled it from its scabbard, regarded it and nodded his approval. He clipped the scabbard to his belt. "When do we go?"

"Now ... there is a footpath from here down the mountain to the main road," Hung Yan told him. "There I have a car in a friend's garage. There is a motorboat waiting at Aberdeen harbour."

The two men left the villa by the rear door, and a few minutes later, Girland found himself on a narrow, dangerously steep path that was shrouded in a damp mist that had come up from the mainland and now blotted out the view.

He moved cautiously, following closely behind Hung Yan. There were moments when he could see nothing, then the mist cleared a little and he caught a glimpse of the Hong Kong lights far below.

Suddenly a stone rattled down behind him, hitting his ankle and he reached out and caught hold of Hung Yan's arm.

"Someone's behind us," he whispered. "You go on ... I'll wait here."

Hung Yan nodded. He continued on down the path. Girland moved off the path down the slope and crouched behind a shrub, his ears pricked, his eyes peering into the half-darkness.

There was a long pause, then he heard the sound of scuffling feet. Peering up, he could make out a small black figure coming cautiously down the path. He waited, tense. The man came on and moved past where Girland was concealed: a small Chinese, his head bent, his movements quick and silent.

Girland pulled himself back onto the path. The man was now ten yards ahead of him. He turned as swiftly as a striking snake when he heard Girland behind him. A knife flashed. Girland went into a low, flying tackle, his arms gripping the man's legs below the knees.

They both crashed down on the path, and slid down in a shower of stones. Hung Yan appeared out of the darkness. He caught the man's wrist as the knife flashed. Girland released his hold and swung a punch at the man's jaw. The blow connected and the man went limp. Before Girland could stop him, Hung Yan had driven his knife into the man's body.

"There may be others," Hung Yan said, his breath hissing between his teeth. "Come on!" He kicked the body off the path and turning, continued down the path.

Girland went after him.

They finally reached the main road without further alarm. Hung Yan led the way across the road to a concrete garage built near a typical Chinese house.

It was as they drove out of the garage in a battered Volkswagen that one of Malik's agents who had lost Girland, spotted the car. He alerted Malik on his walkie talkie.

"Subject heading for Aberdeen harbour," he reported.

Malik looked at Branska and got quickly to his feet.

"Let's go," he said. "The chances are he'll take us right to her."

At the same moment, Wong Loo, the fat Chinese, also received a report. Girland with Hung Yan, he was told, were heading for the harbour. Wong Loo was quite happy about this. He had at least twenty good men in that district. As he sent out directives, he paused to light an American cigarette. Letting the smoke roll out of his thick nostrils, he thought that this was now only a matter of time.

As the wheezy motorboat chugged across the East Lamma Channel, Girland looked back at the hundreds of bobbing lights of the closely packed junks in Aberdeen harbour. He had an instinctive feeling that he was being watched. There was no sign of a following boat, but the feeling persisted.

Hung Yan steered the boat past a Junk that was coming into the harbour, its huge brown sail outlined against the moon. The night was stiflingly hot and the sea oily and calm. The stench of humanity packed in the harbour hung in the air.

As Girland looked across the black expanse of the sea, he saw something moving in the water, close to the boat. He leaned forward, but the movement was gone. A minute later, it appeared again: the fin of a shark that made a swift ripple in the still water and was once again gone. He remembered, when patrolling in the police boat some years ago, the sinister triangle-shaped fins of the sharks that infested this Channel, and he grimaced.

The boat chugged on.

Girland was now aware of the problem facing him. How was he to get this woman out of Hong Kong and back to Paris? he asked himself. It had seemed an easy enough problem when he had accepted the assignment, but now, in this bobbing little boat, he was acutely aware that the Chinese were alert to any move he might make to get the woman out. He thought of Harry Curtis. Harry would help, but then, if he did, Dorey would get to hear about the set up, and that could only lead to more trouble.

Girland thought of the Black Grape ... a half a million dollars for himself! He relaxed and grinned into the darkness. For that money, he should be able to solve the problem. It was wasting time to make plans until he had heard the woman's ideas for escape.

Hung Yan said, "We are getting close," and he reduced the speed of the motorboat. Girland looked around. There were a lot of junks anchored off Pak Kok. Apart from their riding lights, they were in darkness.

Five minutes later, Hung Yan brought the motorboat alongside a big, sailless junk, moored about a half a mile from Pak Kok peninsula, isolated and in darkness.

He whistled softly, and then tied up by the side of the junk. A shadowy figure appeared on the upper deck and peered down at them as they climbed over the side.

"It is all right," Hung Yan called softly. "He is a friend of Carlota's."

The figure climbed down the narrow stairway. In the uncertain light Girland could just make out a tall woman, wearing black Chinese peasant clothes of a baggy coat and trousers and a mushroom-shaped hat.

"Erica Olsen?" he said, peering at her.

"Yes. Come below. Hung ... you stay up here."

The girl went down the five steep steps leading into the cabin and Girland followed her. It was stiflingly hot down there and dark. She closed the door and then striking a match, she lit a small oil lamp.

Sitting at a small table, she took off her hat and shook out her blonde hair.

Girland sat opposite. They stared at each other. He could see the likeness between the sisters, but he saw that Erica was much more beautiful, although she was pale, thin and obviously nervous.

"Give me a cigarette," she said. "I have run out."

Girland pushed his pack across the table. With shaking fingers, she took a cigarette, lit it and then asked, "Did you get me a passport?"

"I got it." Girland handed her the passport. She examined it, then looked up.

"Will it do, do you think?"

"With luck." Girland also lit a cigarette. "Have you any ideas how you will get out?"

"If we can get to the airport, they daren't stop me with you," Erica said. "With any luck they won't even spot me. Have you my ticket?"

"I have an open ticket for the two of us."

She studied him.

"How did you meet Carlota?"

Briefly, Girland told her what had been happening in Paris. She stiffened when he told her he was with the CIA.

"Don't worry your head about that," he said, smiling. "I'm only unofficially attached. They don't know I am out here. I did a deal with your father. For a share in the pearl, I agreed to get you out of here."

"The pearl?"

Girland nodded.

"The Black Grape."

"Oh, for God's sake!" she exclaimed impatiently. "You don't believe that nonsense, do you?"

Girland stiffened, then leaning forward to stare intently at her, he said, "Nonsense? What do you mean?"

"Why do you imagine I am hiding here? Because I stole the Black Grape?"

"Now wait a minute," Girland said, trying to speak calmly. He had a sudden presentiment of disaster. "Carlota told me you had the pearl. She said that was why they were hunting for you." He stabbed his finger at her. "Have you the pearl?"

"Of course not." She flicked ash from her cigarette onto the floor. "My dear man, that was a story I told my sister to get her to co-operate." Her mouth twisted into a bitter smile. "You don't seem to know much about my father and sister. They are two of the most worthless people alive. All they can think about is money. I mean to them as much as a fly on the wall. When I got into this mess, I was desperate as I am desperate now. You can't imagine what it means to be surrounded by Chinese, not knowing if one of them will come out of the crowd and kill you. I was lucky to get this far. Without Hung Yan's help I could never have managed it. Then I found I was trapped. Hung Yan has no influence. I had to get a faked passport. The only two people who could get it for me were my father and sister, but I knew if I didn't offer them a tempting bait they wouldn't do a thing for me. So I told them the story of the Black Grape." She gave a hard little laugh. "The Black Grape is in Kung's museum. An armed guard stands beside the glass case where it is exhibited day and night. There is no possible chance of stealing it. But I didn't tell Carlota this. She swallowed the bait. I had hoped that if she impersonated me in Paris, these thugs hunting for me would give up, but it didn't work out. Do you imagine a woman like Carlota would agree to be tattooed, agree to risk her life unless she was offered an enormous fortune? It was the only possible way I could persuade her to try to save me."

Girland sat back. He crushed out his cigarette as he studied Erica.

"You could be lying, of course," he said without much hope. "You could have the pearl and you're trying to gyp me out of my share."

She met his searching eyes and she shook her head.

"I haven't the pearl ... no one could possibly steal it. It was a story I had to tell Carlota to get me out of here. I am sorry you are disappointed, but I still hope you will help me. You will, won't you?"

"Then if you haven't the pearl, why are they hunting for you? Why are they trying to kill you?"

"Because I know something. You don't sleep with a man for nearly a year without finding out something about him."

"What do you know, Erica?"

She smiled at him.

"Get me out of here and I will tell you, but I am not talking until we are on a plane and out of Hong Kong."

Girland drew in a long deep breath. His rainbow had suddenly vanished into a black cloud. He had been so sure that he was going to be rich. He was now convinced she was telling the truth. It took him a moment or two to shake off the feeling of depression. Then accepting the situation, he shrugged. At least she had some information. So Dorey had been right after all, he thought. That Dorey!

"Well, okay, I'll get you out," he said. "There's no plane before 3 p.m. tomorrow. Have you any clothes?"

"The suitcase I have with me."

"Ah! That solves the mystery of the two suitcases. They told me Carlota had two suitcases when she was in Hong Kong, but only one when she reached Paris. You had the other one?"

"Yes."

Girland thought for a moment.

"As there is no plane until tomorrow afternoon, we had better stay here for the night," he said finally. "We can ..."

He broke off as Erica, staring behind him, suddenly gave a gasping scream. His hand reaching for his knife, Girland whirled around.

"Don't move," Malik said, peering down into the cabin. He held an automatic in his big fist. "Just stay where you are."

He came down the stairs and into the cabin. His huge frame threw a menacing shadow on the wall.

"Oh, for Pete's sake!" Girland exclaimed in disgust. "Can't you keep your long snout out of my business for five minutes? I thought you were safely in Paris."

Malik looked evilly at him.

"It needs very little encouragement for me to put a bullet in you," he said, "so shut up!" He looked at Erica Olsen who was crouching against the far wall, terror in her eyes. "You needn't be frightened of me, Miss Olsen," he went on quietly. "You can regard me as your friend. I overheard what you were saying. I represent the Russian Government. We are very interested in the information you have about

Kung. We can give you far better protection than the American Government. I can assure you there will be no trouble nor risk getting you safely out of Hong Kong and to Moscow. I have a fast motorboat here and a helicopter on the island. There is a chartered aircraft waiting at the airport. Within an hour you will be in complete safety."

Girland looked quickly at Erica. He saw she was getting over her fright and was now studying Malik with a calculating expression in her eyes.

"Don't believe a word of it," he said. "You would be crazy to go to Moscow."

Malik back-handed Girland across his face, sending him staggering against the wall of the cabin.

"I told you to shut up!" he snarled, then to Erica. "He has nothing to offer you, Miss Olsen. He can't help you. He's bluffing. If he is stupid enough to take you on a passenger flight, you will be dead before you even get on the plane."

Erica moved away so she was between Girland and Malik. She studied Malik, then looked at Girland. It was as if she were trying to choose between the two men.

"How do I know you have a chartered plane?" she asked finally.

Malik took a leather folder from his hip pocket and tossed it on the table.

"We fly to Tokyo, avoiding China. From Tokyo we go on to Moscow. If you want proof, here are the plane's papers and the log book."

Erica glanced through the papers, then she nodded.

"All right, I will come with you." She regarded Malik, her eyes shrewd. "I expect to be paid for my information and I expect the price to be high."

"You certainly said it, baby," Girland said. "And it won't be the price you will expect."

She ignored him, still looking at Malik.

"We always pay well for information," Malik said smoothly. "Now please go up on deck. We are leaving immediately. There is a boat waiting with one of my men. Get into the boat."

"Just a moment," Girland said. "What have you done with Hung Yan? Cracked his skull for him?"

"Where is he?" Erica said. "He has helped me. I am not leaving without him."

"He's waiting in the boat," Malik said, his face expressionless. He jerked his thumb to the stairs. "We are wasting valuable time. Please go."

"I have a suitcase."

"I will bring it. Please go!"

Girland said, "He wants you to go because he doesn't want a witness when he murders me."

Erica paused, her eyes searching Malik's face. "It's all right," he said. "I have no reason to kill him. I will leave him here. Will you please go?"

She hesitated no longer and ran up the stairs onto the deck.

Malik backed to the foot of the stairs, then paused, his green eyes glittering.

"I have had enough of your interference, Girland," he said. "I warned you if we ever should meet again I would get rid of you for good. This is an excellent place to leave you." He lifted the automatic. "By the time they find you, we will be in Moscow."

Girland eyed the gun. He felt his mouth suddenly turn dry.

"Don't do anything you might regret later," he said, annoyed his voice sounded husky. "You have the girl. You ..."

The sudden sound of an approaching motorboat coming at high speed made Girland stop. The two men stared at each other in the dim light, both listening. Then there came a crash of gunfire. Malik half-turned, looking up the stairway of the cabin. Girland sprang forward and with a chopping blow on Malik's wrist, sent the gun flying.

Cursing, Malik turned and as he was about to launch himself at Girland there came more gunfire. This was immediately followed by the violent noise of machine-gunfire and the junk rocked under a hail of bullets.

Malik bent to grab his gun, but Girland kicked it into a far corner. Both men stood glaring at each other as more machine-gunfire shook the junk. They heard a thin, wailing scream. Then the motorboat engine roared and began to diminish.

Malik sprang up the stairs and reached the deck. His long knife in his hand, Girland followed him. Both men paused, then Malik raised his clenched fists about his head and cursed.

Erica Olsen was lying flat on her back on the deck, her chest torn open by machine-gun bullets. Already disappearing into the night was a low, fast-moving motorboat heading back to Hong Kong.

Malik spun around and started towards Girland, then seeing the knife in Girland's hand, he paused.

"Come on, Comrade," Girland said quietly. "It will give me a lot of pleasure to slit your throat."

Malik cursed him, then he turned and bent over Erica's body.

"She's dead," he said, straightening. He bent over the side of the junk and looked down at his boat. The crumpled figure of Branska, half-in and half-out of the water told him the machine gun had also caught him.

"We'll have to do something about the Chinese, Malik," Girland said. "While we are fighting each other, they're winning all the tricks." He looked down at Erica's body and grimaced. "I wonder if she did know anything worthwhile about Kung. Maybe she was bluffing. I know the family ... they are great bluffers."

Malik glared at him, his eyes glittering with fury.

"From now on, keep out of my way. If we ever meet again ..."

"Oh, go frighten the Chinese," Girland said impatiently. "Your dialogue's pure ham."

Malik climbed over the side of the junk and lowered himself into the motorboat. He caught hold of Branska and tipped him into the sea, then he started the motorboat engine and not looking back, he headed the boat towards the lights of Hong Kong.

Girland watched him go, then he went to the other side of the junk and made sure his boat was still there. He looked around for Hung Yan, but could see no sign of him. He peered into the moonlit water and saw something move. The long black body of a shark slid by and Girland grimaced. Malik, he thought had probably knocked the Chinese boy over the head and dumped him in the sea.

Girland stood hesitating, then he went down into the stifling cabin. After a quick search, he found Erica's suitcase. He dumped the clothes and the various articles on the cabin floor and went through them carefully. He found nothing of interest. Still hoping he might just be lucky and find the

Black Grape, he slit the lining of the suitcase and eventually took the case to pieces, but he didn't find the pearl.

He wondered if Erica had hidden it in the cabin, but decided she wouldn't have left without it. The only other possible hiding place would be in the clothes she was wearing.

He went up on deck and stood looking down at her body. She was lying in a wide pool of blood. In the moonlight, her chest looked like a big, black hole.

He grimaced. He couldn't bring himself to touch her.

No, the hell with it! he thought. She had been telling the truth. He wasn't going to look further. The whole operation had been a flop from start to finish.

He climbed over the side of the junk into his motorboat, started the engine and headed back to Aberdeen harbour. It was a long and depressing trip and his only companions were the sharks.

An hour later, he shut himself in a telephone booth and put a call through to the Aberdeen Police Station.

A voice with a Scottish accent answered.

"I'm reporting a murder," Girland said. "Junk anchored off Pak Kok. You can't miss it. It isn't carrying a sail. The woman ..."

"Just a moment," the policeman barked. "Who's this talking?"

"The woman's name is Erica Olsen," Girland went on. "The Central Intelligence Agency must be informed. They know about her. She was murdered by Chinese agents acting on orders from Peking."

"Is that so?" the policeman sneered. "If you think I haven't better things to do than to listen to a crackpot ..."

"Shut your fat mouth and listen!" Girland snapped. "Get someone out to that junk if you value your small job," and he hung up.

Leaving the booth, he called a taxi and told the driver to take him to the Lotus Hotel, Wanchai.

Two chattering, giggling Chinese girls were coming out of the hotel as Girland paid off the taxi. They looked invitingly at him, but he didn't notice them. He went up to his room, took a shower and then stretched out on the bed. He thought for some time. The frown on his face showed that his thoughts weren't happy ones. He was blaming himself for Erica's death. Although he had taken precautions, they hadn't been good enough. He had led the Chinese and Malik to the junk. While Malik had been acting out his little scene, the Chinese must have drifted up to the junk, caught Malik's man off guard, spotted Erica on the deck and had let fly at her with a machine gun. At least, they had done their job whereas both Malik and he had failed.

Finally, unable to stand the heat in the little room any longer, his conscience still nagging him, he put on his shabby tropical suit and went downstairs. He took a taxi to the Star Ferry and the steamer to the Kowloon City station and then another taxi to the Hilton Hotel. There he told the receptionist he wanted to put a call through to Monte Carlo. She said there would be a three hour delay. Girland nodded and went to the bar. After three very dry martinis, he felt less depressed and discovered he was hungry. He went down to the grill-room where he ordered a melon with black figs, a blue point steak and a salad with Roquefort dressing. He loitered over the meal, still thinking. The idea of returning to Paris and fooling around with his Polaroid camera was unthinkable. He had Dorey's twenty thousand dollars and the two single air tickets to Paris which he could convert into cash. Not much, but enough and he felt inclined to remain in Hong Kong for a while. Who knows? he thought, cheering up slightly, this is a city of opportunity. I might even find a job out here.

Leaving the restaurant, he returned to the bar. An hour later he was paged and he shut himself into one of the telephone booths.

Olsen came on the line.

"Did you find her?" the voice came faintly over the miles that separated them.

"I found her. I have bad news, Olsen." Girland spoke slowly and distinctly. He wasn't in the mood to have to repeat himself. "She's dead. The Chinese got her first."

"Have you got the Black Grape?" Olsen demanded. Girland smiled wryly. So Erica had been speaking the truth. This fat man was only interested in money. The fact that his daughter was dead meant nothing to him.

"I haven't got it. She never took it. It was a come-on to get Carlota out here. All Erica wanted was to get your co-operation to get her out and she used the Grape as bait."

There was a moment's silence, then Olsen said, his voice rising, "You're lying! You have the pearl and you're trying to gyp me!"

"Oh, relax! She never got near it. It's guarded night and day. She found out some top secret stuff about Kung and they silenced her."

"Do you expect me to believe that?" Olsen screamed. "You're lying! Now listen, you cheap crook, you either hand me the pearl in exactly three days' time or that tape goes to Dorey and he'll then learn what a goddamn crook you are. Do you hear me?"

"Get your mind off money," Girland said, his own voice rising. "Do you realise your daughter's dead?"

"Do you think I care about that little bitch!" Olsen yelled. "You give me the pearl in three days' time or the tape goes to Dorey," and he slammed down the receiver.

Girland stared at himself in the tiny mirror above the telephone. He grimaced, shaking his head at himself. This time, he felt, Olsen wasn't bluffing. He shrugged and walked back to the bar. He sat down, ordered a large whisky on the rocks and stared bleakly out of the big window, overlooking the busy waterfront.

Well, that settles it for me, he thought. If Dorey gets that tape, he'll blow his stack. I'll have to stay here until Paris cools off ... if it ever cools off.

He paid for his drink, sipped it and relaxed back in his chair. Maybe he had better keep one of the air tickets, he said to himself. Sooner or later, he would want to return to Paris. The Lotus Hotel was very cheap. He could remain in Hong Kong if he were careful for a couple of months. He felt himself relaxing. He had the facility of shedding unpleasant experiences very quickly. He suddenly found himself looking forward to those two months. He suddenly didn't want to sit in this luxury bar for the rest of the evening with his thoughts. Carrying his glass he went back to the telephone booths. He gave the telephonist the Lotus hotel number. When Wan See came on the line, Girland said, "There's a girl I'm interested in. Her name's Tan-Toy. Where can I contact her?"

"Is that Mr Girland?"

"Who else did you think it was?"

"Yes, I know her. She has a room on Jaffe Road."

"Is that near you?"

"A hundred yards."

"Would you send someone round there? Tell her I'm at the Hilton, and I want to see her. Will you do that?"

"Yes, with pleasure."

"The pleasure will be mine I hope, but thanks."

Girland carried his glass back to the bar and sat down. He believed that life should never be wasted. It was short enough as it is, he reasoned. The trick of living a full life was to make good use of every hour.

Crossing his long legs, he settled down to wait for Tan-Toy to come to him.

James Hadley Chase

An Ace Up My Sleeve

When three very different people come together, all out for the same thing and prepared to go to any lengths to get it, the stakes are likely to be high. But, for a wealthy middle-aged woman, an international lawyer and a young American, games of bluff and counter-bluff quickly develop into a dangerous and deadly battle. As the action hots up, Chase weaves a fast-moving story of blackmail, intrigue and extortion with a hair-raising climax.

The Fast Buck

International jewel thief, Paul Hater, knows a secret that everyone wants to know – and will go to any lengths to uncover. How long can he remain silent?

When Hater is arrested in possession of a stolen necklace, the police use every possible means to persuade him to reveal the location of the rest of the collection. He remains silent and so begins his twenty-year prison sentence. Having exhausted all their leads, the International Detective Agency, acting on behalf of the insurers, must patiently await Hater's release before they can hope to find out more. But just as his day of release approaches, Hater is kidnapped by a ruthless international gang determined to force the secret from him and prepared to go to any lengths to do so...

James Hadley Chase

Have a Change of Scene

Larry Carr is a diamond expert in need of a break. So when his psychiatrist suggests he has a change of scene, he jumps at the opportunity to move to Luceville, a struggling industrial town, and become a social worker. This, he thinks, will give him all the rest he needs...until he runs into Rhea Morgan, a ruthless, vicious thief who also happens to be extremely attractive. He falls headlong into the criminal world and embarks upon a thrilling, rapid and dastardly adventure in true Hadley Chase style.

Just a Matter of Time

An old lady's will seems to be causing quite a stir. Suddenly everyone wants to get in on the action, everyone that is, including a master forger, a hospital nurse, a young delinquent, a bank executive and, to make matters worse, a professional killer. With such ingredients, a showdown seems inevitable and James Hadley Chase adds enough suspense to keep you guessing right up to the very last page.

James Hadley Chase

My Laugh Comes Last

Farrell Brannigan, President of the National Californian Bank, is an extremely successful man. So when he builds another bank in an up-and-coming town on the Pacific coast, he is given worldwide publicity, and this new bank is hailed as 'the safest bank in the world'. But Brannigan's success came at a price and he made many enemies on his way up the ladder. It seems that one of them is now set on revenge and determined to destroy both the bank and Brannigan himself.

You're Dead Without Money

Joey Luck and his daughter Cindy were small-time criminals going nowhere fast...until they joined forces with Vin Pinna, a hardened criminal on the run from Miami. They began to set their sights higher and turned their hands to kidnapping. But their hostage, ex-movie star Don Elliot, seemed to have different ideas. He wanted in so they formed a 'quartet in crime' and this time the stakes were higher still – eight Russian stamps worth a million dollars.

'realistic and suspenseful' – *Observer*